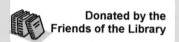

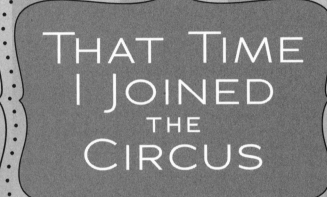

THAT TIME
I JOINED
THE
CIRCUS

THAT TIME
I JOINED
THE
CIRCUS

J. J. HOWARD

Point

Library of Congress Cataloging-in-Publication Data

Howard, J. J. (Jennifer Jane), 1972-
That time I joined the circus / J.J. Howard. — 1st ed.
p. cm.
Summary: After her father's sudden death and a break-up with her best friends, seventeen-year-
old Lexi has no choice but to leave New York City seeking her long-absent mother, rumored to
be in Florida with a traveling circus, where she just may discover her destiny.
ISBN 978-0-545-43381-5
[1. Circus — Fiction. 2. Best friends — Fiction. 3. Friendship — Fiction. 4. Single-parent families —
Fiction. 5. Mothers and daughters — Fiction. 6. Florida — Fiction. 7. New York (N.Y.) — Fiction.]
I. Title.
PZ7.H83296Th 2013
[Fic] — dc23
2012016715

10 9 8 7 6 5 4 3 2 1   13 14 15 16 17/0

Printed in the U.S.A.   23
First edition, April 2013
Book design by Christopher Stengel

From bonding over
Roswell to being stuck
together all the time in
1120 and 7 and 8, thanks,
BFF—for everything.

THAT TIME
I JOINED
THE
CIRCUS

PROLOGUE

"A detour to your new life
Tell all of your friends good-bye"
— BROKEN BELLS, "THE HIGH ROAD"

The Corner of Bowery and Rivington — Tuesday, October 5

My life has a soundtrack — it plays in my head all the time. Sometimes it's on automatic, just a song stuck on repeat from the last thing I listened to. And sometimes I'm like a DJ, making a selection to suit my mood or the general circumstance. When there's music playing in the outside world, though, sometimes it takes over. Like now.

My father taught me about music, which is how I know that the sound coming out of the bar called Mission doesn't qualify. I think it's Nickelback, or someone who was on, like, *American Idol*, but it's completely beneath me to know for sure. I am a music snob, and proud of it. I'm a New Yorker; smugness is my birthright. But being alone, cold, and hungry — and homeless as of around ten o'clock this morning — has taken some of the smug out of me. I never thought I'd live anywhere but New York — never even thought I'd live above Houston Street.

1

Maybe if I hadn't messed up quite so completely, one of my two (former) best friends would be standing here with me. Maybe if I'd actually bothered to learn how to drive . . . maybe if my dad hadn't died . . . But no maybes would help: I had, I hadn't, he had.

So here I am saying good-bye to my neighborhood, alone, with no plan beyond the bus station and a really crummy song about love stuck in my head. And of course my stupid mother to go and find. What kind of father sends all his money to his crazy ex-wife and leaves his daughter completely broke? And what kind of mother runs away and joins the circus?

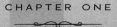

CHAPTER ONE

ELI

"Should I feel flattered that you hate everything but me?"
— MARITIME, "PARADE OF PUNK ROCK T-SHIRTS"

—

Orchard Street and Avenue A — Thursday, September 30

Eli won — again. He's my best friend, but that doesn't make it any less annoying. We were sitting on the floor of his bedroom, which is not that easy, because his room is even smaller than mine. I had just lost seventeen dollars and forty-two cents playing five-card draw. We were trying to stay awake to see a midnight showing of *Robot Monster* at the Den of Cin on Avenue A. And waiting for Bailey to arrive. Things had been pretty weird since Eli and Bailey — my two best friends — my two only friends, to be completely accurate — started dating each other a few months ago. Having Eli all to myself that night had actually been kind of nice. Being the odd freak out had not been all that awesome.

Eli Katz and I have been friends since we started at Sheldon in sixth grade. I'd gone to public school for elementary, and Eli had gone to a little yeshiva down the street.

Neither of us fit the Sheldon Prep mold very well. I had a dad who looked like a teenager in his D G A: Now START A BAND T-shirt and a missing mother. Eli had strict parents and almost never ventured more than three blocks from his apartment. My dad, Gavin, and I taught him to be almost as obsessive about music as we are. Gavin even taught him to play the guitar, which was a big improvement over the clarinet he'd been trying to play when I met him.

Eli and I hated the Sheldon kids — that is, until Bailey Conners came along in ninth. Bailey was pretty enough, and naturally non-awkward enough — and wealthy enough — to fit in with the typical Sheldon kids. But for some unknown reason, she picked us instead. Eli and I had both been flattered and kind of grateful.

It took me a little while to figure out what it was about Bailey. She certainly looked like someone who could have her own show on The CW. But she didn't quite fit in with the shiny people at Sheldon. The day she brought the pigeon with the smashed wing to class with her (in a Jimmy Choo shoe box, no less), I started to figure it out. She had a soft spot for wounded birds. Bailey has a good heart, and she loves a project. Her makeover scheme had worked on Eli, at least.

And I guess if I am honest with myself, I had seen right away that Eli's feelings about Bailey hadn't stopped at gratitude. When Bailey spoke, Eli's head always tilted to the side, and he gazed at her sort of like a faithful hound dog.

"X? Call?" Eli's voice brought me back to the game.

"Fold." I threw in my cards with a huge sigh. "You've got my popcorn money, and my download budget for at least the next two weeks."

"Try two days, addict."

"You're so funny!" I said in my best fake voice. "For a retarded person, I mean."

Eli threw his cards at me, but he smiled. "Clean up that mess you made, will ya?"

I leaned back against the side of his bed, stretching my legs while keeping them crossed in my little skirt. I hated shorts, but it was about 112 degrees out, and a little skirt was my only other option. Eli was wearing jeans, as always. I watched him gather up the cards I'd known he wouldn't make me pick up. Eli was so different now — the way he filled out his T-shirt was such a change from the old string bean he'd been. It was hot in his room — his parents definitely rationed the air-conditioning — and I gathered all my hair up and held it on top of my head for a few seconds, wishing for a hair clip. It was getting really long. Probably time to cut it. I didn't actually hate my hair — it was sort of medium brown, but thick with a little wave to it. It was just too bad I hadn't inherited Gavin's light blue, almost silver eyes. Mine were just regular blue.

As I watched Eli put away the cards, I was startled by the jolt of my cell phone in the side pocket of my skirt. I slid the answer bar and asked, "Hi, what are you doing?"

Gavin, I mouthed to Eli's questioning look. My dad was not the sort of dad that my friends called Mr. Ryan. I started calling him Gavin a long time ago to annoy him, and then it sort of stuck.

Wherever my dad was, there was synthpop in the background. This was not exactly unusual. My dad is stuck somewhere in the late eighties. He visits me here in the post-millennium, but that's not where he really lives.

"Where are you?" he asked.

"Eli's."

"Shock. I thought you were gonna be home early tonight, though?"

"When did I say that?" Gavin often got things scrambled.

"I thought you had that college fair thing."

"Oh — *last* night. I went. No sweat. Already picked my school. The University of Kentucky. I'm looking into maybe getting some horses."

"I was supposed to go with you." He really did sound contrite.

"That's okay." I was mostly telling the truth. Gavin was an awesome dad, but not so big on the nuts-and-bolts stuff.

"I was working — I totally forgot. I'm sorry, Lexi."

I didn't correct him — Lexi was his pet name for me. He mostly obeyed my wish to be called Xandra now. As long as I didn't have to be Alex, like that idiot Mr. Rosso, my chemistry teacher, insisted on calling me. When I tried to correct him, he said there are no proper names that start with an X.

"So . . . horses. Got it. I have to say, I kind of thought you'd go NYU, maybe Columbia. But, you know, Kentucky, that's cool, too."

"You wouldn't think it was cool if you had to buy the horse," I told him as I watched Eli flip open his laptop and stretch out diagonally across his bed. "What's up, Gavin? Did you need something? It doesn't sound like you're even home."

"My name is *Dad*. And no, I was calling about that school thing that I already missed. When will you be home?"

"Before you, probably. Be good, though."

"I will if you will." I heard the click. The man wasn't big on good-byes.

"What did Gavin want?" Eli asked, looking up from his screen. His head was close to mine, hanging over the edge of the bed.

"Just checking in. I need caffeine. I don't think I'll make it through *Robot Monster*. I think I'm gonna head."

"That's too bad," Eli said, his face aimed back down at the screen. "Bailey just messaged me; she's bailing on us."

I had a weird feeling — a sudden conviction, actually — right at that moment that I should get up off Eli's floor and go straight home. Eli looked down at me, and I saw something mischievous in his eyes and a lock of dark hair falling over his left eye. When did he get so freaking cute? Why was this my life?

If only I'd listened to that weird premonition, the worst night of my life would have been a tiny bit less horrible.

I stood up, but then I sat back down on the bed, with my legs over Eli's legs, my back against the wall behind his bed. Eli turned over and looked at me for a minute. When he spoke, his voice was pitched low; his eyes still held mine. "So, what do you want to do now?"

I didn't make it home that night at all. I wish more than anything that I had.

CHAPTER TWO

NOTE TO SELF: PACK MORE KLEENEX

"And if you feel just like a tourist in the city you were born
Then it's time to go"
— DEATH CAB FOR CUTIE, "YOU ARE A TOURIST"

The Middle of Freaking Nowhere — Thursday, October 7

I sat on a Greyhound bus, heading, on purpose, to somewhere in the middle of Florida. There was a chance my mother would be there when I arrived, but I had no way of knowing.

This was probably what I deserved.

My dad's lawyer was the one who made me realize that I had to leave New York. He shook his head. A lot. He talked about investments that hadn't panned out, about Dad being overextended. I had trouble following his words. The soundtrack in my head was just static.

The deal was that my dad had a little bit of money left, and Max, his lawyer, had sent it on to my mom, because that was the arrangement Dad had made. "It wasn't easy," he told me, leaning back in his fancy chair. The rest of the office wasn't that fancy; it was on Avenue B, wedged in between a hot pretzel stand and a tattoo parlor. "Your mother moves around a great deal. In fact" — he wasn't looking at me; he was playing with the Roberto Alomar bobblehead on his desk — "she's actually on the move now. She's with a circus that's working a circuit down south."

"Working at a *circus?* Are you seriously telling me she *joined the circus?*"

He handed me a slip of paper; I looked down at the address, but my brain didn't process the writing on it as words.

"Your mother's always performed," he said matter-of-factly, as though to combat the freak-out I was starting to have by being super calm. He still wasn't looking at me; now he was fiddling with his shirtsleeves, which he unrolled only to reroll. "At any rate, I tracked down the address for you — even made some calls to find out where they'd be. If you leave New York by the weekend, you should arrive just as the show does."

"Um, okay . . ." I stood up and paced around his small office. "I mean, I guess I don't actually have much of a choice here."

I had already tried going to Sheldon Prep to try to liquidate my assets — since my dad had prepaid, I thought maybe I could get that money back, live on it, and go to public school to finish high school. But the headmistress said no way. In fact, even though I was enrolled and paid, she said she'd need a letter from either my mom or a foster parent before I could even come back. What a sweetheart.

And getting a job and finding my own place in the city was not gonna happen. I personally knew about ten adults who lived around my neighborhood who were desperately looking for work. A seventeen-year-old with absolutely no experience and no useful skills didn't have the slightest chance. And the rent on my dad's apartment, though it was reasonable for the area, was $1950. A month. I had maybe twenty-seven dollars to my name, and no way to get any more. The landlord gave me a few days' grace. Which was actually pretty nice of him.

So it really didn't matter whether I wanted to leave or that I thought chasing after some circus sounded like the stupidest thing in the world to do. This slip of paper in my hand was it. All I had.

"It's not so bad," I heard Max saying. "I mean, I'm sure once you find your mother, it will all be fine."

"Yeah," I told him. But I was lying. I walked out of Max's office in a daze.

How had this *happened*? Gavin wasn't much of a planner, but this was ridiculous. Had he expected my mom to just magically appear to take care of me if he ever couldn't? It probably never even occurred to him that he wouldn't always be there. Or that without enough money to pay even one month of rent, I was going to be evicted and penniless pretty fast. But thinking about my dad being gone was making it hard to breathe, and so I stopped. I was not ready. Not yet. Besides, I had too much to deal with to let myself fall apart.

I was also more than a little bit afraid that when I let myself think about this whole thing too much, I was not only going to miss my dad, but be really ticked off at him for leaving me with nothing. I had always known that Gavin was not big on the boring, necessary life stuff. I had been the one to pay the electric bill since I was thirteen — well, *arrange* the payment with a check from Gavin's checkbook. We'd had our power cut off so many times that I had decided to take over. He had left me so much worse than in the dark this time.

But the Greyhound bus was because of *her.*

I hate my mom. I mean, people say that, but I actually mean it. Like all the time, not just in a moment of anger for being grounded or something. I actually hate her. She left me and my dad, and she never looked back. And if I didn't miss Gavin so much, and if I didn't feel like I was going to rip in half every time I started to think about him, maybe I'd hate him, too, for making me come to find her, leaving me with no other way to actually survive.

I did think, for one second before getting on that first bus, about giving up. Just not caring, not bothering to find my mom, just sitting down in the street and being done.

But just for one second. For some stupid reason, I guess I actually cared about my miserable, ridiculous life.

The bus was very hot, but there were only about four other passengers, and nothing to look at out the window. My eyes started to burn, and it hurt to swallow. I tried to think of stuff I could remember without crying. I would not — would *not* — think about the last week, so I went back further. Halloween — last Halloween — seemed like a good place to start. That was my dad's favorite holiday, and mine, too, I guess.

I was getting ready to go out. Eli was taking me to see a Dead Milkmen cover band. I was really excited about my costume; I was turning myself into the gargoyle above the apartments near the library branch building on 10th. I was painting my face gray and attaching prosthetic elf ears while my dad blasted Ministry's "Everyday Is Halloween" on his big speakers. He was in the kitchen making potato pancakes, which for some reason he made every Halloween. The apartment was loud and smelled like food. I grinned into the mirror and my gray face grinned back.

"Lex!" I heard Gavin yell from the kitchen. "Come taste the batter!"

I gathered up the sheet that I was still fashioning into my costume and mummy-shuffled to the kitchen. "Coming!" I yelled, tasting some of the face paint I had applied too liberally around my mouth.

I spit into the kitchen sink as soon as I got there.

"Aw, Lex, gross — you haven't even tasted them yet!"

After some more spitting I accepted the glass of water Dad held out to me. "I'm gonna need some help spray-painting my body," I told him.

"As long as you mean the sheet *covering* your body, I'm in. Otherwise, we are going to have to go get Mrs. Murchison from downstairs."

I narrowed my eyes at him. "Do you mean to say that you'd let me go out in nothing but body paint?"

Gavin laughed. "If I thought there was any chance you'd ever do that, maybe I'd worry about trying to prevent it."

I flounced inelegantly onto a bar stool. "I hate being so predictable! I should make you worry — and have gray hair! It's like my job as your child, and I just can't help but feel I'm failing you."

He added some pepper to his batter and stirred. "My mother did promise me, many times, that when I had a child of my own, I'd have to deal with even worse behavior than mine, and then I'd see . . . But" — he looked at me for a moment — "nah, nope, never had to worry with you. My mother was so totally wrong!" Gavin triumphantly spooned up some pancake batter and zoomed the spoon toward my mouth.

"Ew, Dad, how many times do I have to tell you I hate uncooked batter?" I swallowed the raw potato liquid, sputtering and resisting the urge to wipe my mouth (in honor of my makeup).

"Sorry, Lex, I forgot. See, again, you are so proper. You won't eat the cookies until they are *properly* baked at the *proper* temperature . . ."

I glared back at him. "Cookie batter, maybe, but potato's

disgusting. I'm sure they'll be awesome when they're cooked, though!" I hurried to add when I saw his face.

But Dad grinned again. "Yes, when they have been cooked *properly*."

I jumped down from the stool, and one of my ears fell off, which only made him laugh harder at me.

"How your mother and I ever had such a good kid, I will never know," he observed, not for the first time.

"I'm sorry to be such a disappointment to you." I lowered my gray head.

I felt Dad's hand under my chin; he was gentle, so as not to smudge me. "I've never been disappointed in you," he said, suddenly serious. "I thought you knew that."

I smiled at him, words failing me, and blinking hard so no tears would damage my face.

"Now, when's Eli picking you up?"

"Like, an hour."

"Good. Go get me whatever you use to take off makeup. Get me all of it."

"What do you mean?"

Dad put his hands on my shoulders and looked right at me, his light silver eyes serious once more. "Lex, child of mine, I love you. And I applaud your creativity. But, sweetheart, you look ridiculous in that getup. I think it's time for the emergency costume closet."

I blinked for a second, saw he was serious, and tried to swallow my pride. One hour!

I ended up going out in some of his and my mom's old punk stuff. My feelings were pretty hurt at the time, but now I was thinking he probably saved me from a lot more embarrassment.

I noticed then that the lady next to me on the bus was staring at me, like she was trying to figure out whether or not to ask me if I was okay. So much for stuff I can remember without crying.

Somewhere in the Carolinas, I don't know which one, I started to think of less-happy memories. I only had two pocket-pack tissues left to last me all the way to Florida.

For one thing, there's singing, or more precisely, not singing. I actually have a pretty decent voice — no surprise, since my mother used to sing professionally, mostly in clubs and at events. She made an album when I was a toddler, but she never got a recording deal or anything. And my dad can — could — sing, too. He had a band when I was little, Vinyl Parade, and although he wasn't the lead singer, he sang harmony and background and stuff.

My mom used to sing around the house all the time, and I used to, too. After she left it was quiet, so quiet it hurt to breathe, and it was hard to speak; when I wanted to say something to my dad, I planned it all out in my head, and then for some reason the words still felt stuck, like when I was learning to dive and I would get ready and stand on the end of the board and then freeze, waiting, not sure I was ready to take the plunge. After weeks and weeks like this, I remember one day just bursting out into song, like I was a Disney cartoon or something. I was washing the dishes and I'd thought Gavin was in his room, but then he appeared in the kitchen doorway, and he gave me this look — I'll never forget it — angry and sad and just, like, lost.

"Lexi, stop." That's all he said.

And so I did; I stopped. I never sang another note, not ever again.

Thanks, Mom and Dad.

CHAPTER THREE

THE SUNSHINE STATE

"Here I am, a rabbit-hearted girl
Frozen in the headlights"
— FLORENCE + THE MACHINE, "RABBIT HEART (RAISE IT UP)"

Somewhere in the Middle of Florida—Friday, October 8

I ended up in an empty field, standing in a sponge.

That's what it felt like: standing down in one of the little holes of a kitchen sponge. The air was actually wet.

I sat down on top of the suitcase that contained my worldly goods. I don't know how long I sat there before two big trucks pulled up and parked in the field. A couple of minutes later, a door on the side of one of the trucks clanged open. I saw hands lowering a set of metal stairs, and then probably the owner of those hands tumbled down the stairs a few seconds later.

The man was maybe a little shorter than me, with dark black hair slicked back and tied into a short, neat ponytail at the base of his neck. He wore a red button-down shirt that looked a bit worse for wear with the sleeves rolled up and black pants. As he came close to me, I stood up, knocking over my suitcase in the process.

"Who are you?" he demanded. He had a strong Eastern Europe–flavored accent. "Suitcases! Of course! Always they are showing up here with suitcases. And hard-luck stories. Have you brought one of those as well?"

Well, welcome to the freaking circus.

"You could say that," I said, trying to get my bag to sit upright on the sandy ground. "But actually I'm here looking for my mother, I guess."

"You guess? Is this some kind of game?"

"No. I mean, it's not a game. I am looking for her. I wish I weren't, but that's not your problem." He sort of snorted at that, but it wasn't an entirely unfriendly sound. Maybe he was glad I wasn't trying to lay my baggage — literal and figurative — on him.

"My name is Xandra," I continued. "My mom was supposed to be here. Her name is Callie Ryan. Or maybe Thompson." The guy gave me a look, but I didn't blink. It wasn't my fault my mother was a rotten liar whose own kid didn't actually know for sure what her name was these days.

"I think I had a Callie on board for a time ... or a Connie — no, it was definitely Callie." The man regarded me thoughtfully. "But it's been six months at least since she left. People come and they go around here." He shrugged, then abruptly started walking past me.

"Hold on a second!" I raced to catch up with him. If this rude guy left, I would have zero in the way of leads on finding my mom. And no money to, like, live.

The man turned. "I told you Callie's moved on." He

sounded genuinely puzzled about why I was still talking to him.

"I know, but . . . isn't there anything else you can tell me? I mean, I really, really need to find her. I don't really have another option here. I wish I did, but I just don't. Did she leave anything behind, like an address? Or is there somebody else here who worked with her maybe?"

He shook his head. "I haven't the time to question my people about a woman who worked here for less than one season. Sorry." He turned to go again.

"*Wait!* Seriously, dude. I mean . . . sir. What you said about the hard luck. I mean, I'm sure you've heard about hard luck. But mine is really . . . hard. We're talking granite, or like a diamond or something. Wait, that sounds kind of positive." He sighed, and I knew I was losing my audience. "I can work! I mean, can I work? Here? For you here? I could do anything. I just need to sort of . . . eat at some point. And I could maybe find out some more about where my momster might have gone."

"I knew it!" He slapped his leg for emphasis. "As soon as I saw the bags, I knew. All right . . . but you must promise to stay until the end of the season. Even if you find a lead on this mother of yours. Until December. You make solemn vow — yes?"

I nodded. "Yes! I mean, thank you, yes."

"You may wish you hadn't thanked me when I give you your first job. I am Louie Vrana," he said, extending his hand and shaking mine once, very forcefully. "The animals arrive tonight," he told me over his shoulder as he resumed walking. "Put your things in that truck with the stairs. You can rest on the couch in there. You will need it."

Turns out I was more bus-tired than I thought, because I curled up on Louie's couch and drifted off.

I fell asleep in an empty field, but I woke up at the circus.

I stumbled down the little metal stairs and almost walked into a tiger. Yes, a bright-orange-and-black striped, majestic tiger. Thankfully, he had a rope around his neck and was being led by an old man in grubby corduroy overalls. The man glared at me and it sounded like he cursed, though not in English or even a language I recognized. I mumbled an apology. I could walk through the subway station at Forty-second Street at rush hour without running into anyone, but here in the middle of nowhere, I almost trip over a tiger.

The animal appeared to pay me no mind and kept striding ahead, its muscles rippling.

I looked around. In addition to the tiger guy, I saw two women leading horses in a circle. I'd never seen — or smelled — so many animals up close before. I'd seen them on television, at zoos, in movies, but this was different. I felt very tiny and crushable.

The two big trucks had become five. I saw a bunch of people leading an elephant slowly down one of the ramps. The elephant looked sort of grumpy and grubby, kind of like the tiger man. It was a muddy brown-gray color, and even from across the field I could smell a distinct odor that must be elephant specific, sort of a mix of grass and wet dog.

I sat down on the stairs. Between the sleep deprivation and being about ten feet from an *elephant*, I felt really weird. I was also starting to understand that my life was getting very surreal very fast. Here I was, over a thousand miles from home, at the *circus*, sitting here gaping at an elephant, two horses, and a tiger.

And holding a shovel. A boy who looked like he was maybe in middle school walked up to me and handed it to me without a word. I stood up, but he was already walking away.

"Wait up!" I yelled after the boy. He stopped, but still didn't speak. "I guess I'm supposed to help you?" I asked him.

He grunted. I guessed that was a yes.

"What's your name?" He stopped and spun around. Close up, I thought maybe he was older than I'd originally thought, but I couldn't really tell because he was covered in dirt.

"Costi," he said, then turned and resumed walking.

"So what are we doing?" I asked him. When he didn't answer, I just kept following him. He led me up the ramp of the elephant truck and into an open cage.

It turned out Costi wasn't covered in dirt.

He demonstrated briefly what to do. It wasn't exactly a complicated procedure. Then he left me to it, going back down the ramp and presumably into one of the other trucks.

I started shoveling, trying not to smell — or breathe. My shoulders and hands hurt after only a few minutes. I kept waiting for the temperature to drop now that the sun had gone down, but it was still hot and humid, which wasn't helping with the smell situation. I wished I had a scarf or something to wipe the sweat from my hairline, but I had to make do with the hem of my T-shirt.

Costi came back to check my work and silently helped me finish off the rest of the elephant cage. Then we went on to the truck the tigers had arrived in. We kept working, and I found creative ways to hold my breath. Around us, small trailers and cars kept pulling in. When the cages were finally clean, about nine thousand smelly shovelfuls later, I followed Costi back toward the center of the field. I rubbed my poor right shoulder and tried to remember if I'd packed Tylenol.

A whole circus city was being built right before my eyes. A lighted path led to a round section of the field that had been cleared. Some of the smaller trucks were already parked in their places, ready to open as concession stands or ticket booths. Someone had set up a pair of huge speakers, and "Hotel California" was playing as Costi and I walked by.

We landed at a line of horse trailers. It seemed that the girl who usually took care of the horses hadn't shown up, if I interpreted Costi's grunts correctly, so he brushed and fed them while grunting orders at me. I filled buckets and buckets of water from the hose someone had hooked up, carried feed bags, and tried to lift with my legs.

The people who came to claim each animal seemed to share Costi's tendency to go about their work without speaking. But as more of the crew — "the ring crew," I heard someone say — began to show up, I found out that silence was not everyone's way here. I counted twelve guys and one girl — everyone introduced themselves — and their names were almost all common American names, so I promptly got confused as to who was who. One particularly boisterous guy, Doug, was memorable. Michael Jackson's "Thriller" started playing, and he kept singing along (off-key) and trying to do the zombie dance. Everyone laughed at him, me included.

The one crew girl, Heather, told me they were setting up the rows of seats around the center ring. She wasn't quite as dirty as me, but her Orlando Magic T-shirt was ripped and stained, and her blond hair was piled on top of her head in a messy bun. I sat down in the grass while the seats were set up. It seemed pretty clear that we weren't done, though I was almost afraid to ask what came next. I didn't have to, though; Heather told me.

"Don't fall asleep, new girl. The real work's the tent. Everybody helps with that part."

Indeed, everyone who wasn't attached to a tiger or a horse turned up to help lay out the gigantic red canvas. All around the circle we held the edges of the material as the crew set the poles and finally tied the tent in place.

I lifted my arms in the air, holding up my little corner of the tent. When I could finally let go and look at my watch, I saw it had been just an hour, but it had felt like a hundred. My arms felt numb, and I would have given anything for a shower.

"Who's that guy?" I asked Heather. The tent was up, but one guy kept on circling it, tightening and adjusting the ropes, and barking orders at people.

"That's Carl — the tent master." Heather didn't seem inclined to explain, but another one of the guys came up behind me.

"The tent is kinda the heart of the operation," the older man told me. "We've gotta get it right. Especially here — gets pretty windy in Florida. This your first time on a show, huh?" he asked. "I'm Joe, by the way."

I nodded. "Hi, Joe," I said. "It's that obvious, huh?"

He smiled. "You're doing fine," he said. "Everybody's gotta start somewhere."

I thanked him and he walked away. Most of the crew I'd been working with had begun to wander off, but I didn't know if I was free yet, so I sat back down and looked around. Beyond the tent, rows and rows of carefully parked trailers were lit from within. The nicest trailers were closest to the tent — some were big, probably bigger than our old apartment. I saw a dark-haired girl glide down the steps of one of the nicer ones. From her posture and the grace of her walk I immediately pegged her for a dancer — live in New York long enough and you get to know what dancers look like.

Heather flopped down beside me. "Who is that?" I asked her.

"That's Lina. Her dad's Louie — the guy who hired you. He's the boss."

Lina walked toward us and I smiled at her. She didn't smile back.

"She's probably some kind of dancer?" I said to Heather as she sailed past us.

"Close," she said, lighting a cigarette. "Flying trapeze."

"I was gonna guess that next," I told her.

Eventually, everyone started to clear out. "Bunk's this way," Heather told me. "Unless you have your own trailer?"

"I came here on a Greyhound," I told her.

"Me too," Heather said. "The rest of the crew trailer's all guys, but they're okay. As long as you don't mind snoring." I watched Heather stamp out her cigarette under her booted heel. She didn't seem to think there was anything weird about rooming with twelve guys. I looked around at them. They all looked pretty exhausted and harmless, but the idea still freaked me out. I followed her to the very back of the lot, then up the steps into a huge trailer. Once inside, I saw there were rows of beds stacked two high on both sides.

Most of them had sheets or scraps of fabric hung up as privacy curtains.

"Welcome home, new girl. This bunk's up for grabs." Heather gestured to one that didn't have a curtain, then climbed into one a little farther down and unceremoniously yanked her curtain shut.

There was nothing else left to do. I climbed onto the tiny, creaky bed. I curled away from the center aisle. My clothes were filthy, and I smelled like elephants and tigers and oh, my . . . But my bag was back in Louie's trailer, and it seemed like I'd need to wait until morning to get it back.

I tried not to think of home, or of hot showers or clean pajamas, or of someone who cared if I ever had those things again. I lay there as guys trickled in and started to settle down. It got quiet pretty fast. But soon the chorus of snoring started. I got up and crept back outside.

The night was dark and not any cooler. The strange little circus town I'd helped to build blurred in my vision, and through the tears I imagined for a moment that the lights I could see were the lights of New York City. I shivered and imagined it was from the cold. If only wishing could make any of it so. But when I wiped my eyes, the air was still warm: I was still at the circus. I had to stop wishing — I had nowhere else to go.

I sat on the steps of the trailer for a long time. Alone.

CHAPTER FOUR

I Don't Mind, or I'm Just Good at Pretending I Don't

*"In my heart, I've always known
I gotta be happy alone"*
— Earlimart, "Happy Alone"

—

13 Broome Street — Friday, May 14

Bailey almost tripped over me, then she leaned down, ponytail bouncing. "Hey, girl! What's shaking?"

Sitting on the floor watching everyone stream past me, or step over me, without even noticing I was there was only mildly depressing at this point. I'd been fading into the antique woodwork at the Sheldon Upper School since freshman year. Bailey, though, always got noticed. There had been a couple of freshman guys sitting opposite me for the past twenty minutes — I think one was copying the other's algebra homework. They stopped "working" and stared at Bailey.

"Nothing's shaking; just glad last period's finally over. How was bio?" I asked.

"Well, it smells like evil in there, as always. But we did group work, and I got to sit with Dana Marsters — you know, the senior? She's retaking bio. Anyway, it was awesome! She invited me to lunch this weekend and everything."

"Swell." I tried to smile. As far as I was concerned, if there was an aroma of evil in the bio lab, it was coming from Dana Marsters. But Bailey sees the good in everybody, and she is almost always in a good mood. It takes some getting used to. Eli and I used to be more dark-cloudy, but with Bailey the sun is always shining.

"And now we get to go shopping!" Bailey did a little hopping dance and sang the word *shopping*.

"I thought you and Eli were going out tonight."

"Duh, it's Friday. But we have hours until then. I want to get a new dress."

Bailey wanted to get a new dress for every day ending in *y*, so this was not a surprise.

"Sure, I'll go with," I heard myself saying. Watching Bailey try on fifty dresses, most of them twice, for her date tonight was not really what I'd had in mind for my afternoon. But since all of my plans had involved me, by myself, at my apartment . . .

Plus, Bailey was already pulling me toward the door. "Knew I could count on you." She smiled. Bailey always wins. The force of her enthusiasm connects with my ambivalence, and we go where she was heading anyway.

I told Bailey I'd meet her outside in five. I had to stash my books in the art room. Sheldon Prep is so old, and looks so much like an old mansion — probably because it once was one — that it doesn't have lockers. So my shoulder was breaking from carrying every single book I owned. My algebra II and chem books each weighed about a hundred pounds.

Sheldon has block schedules: block like cell block. Basically most of my day might as well be taught in a foreign language; I don't speak math. Four hours a day of math — I'm pretty sure the state is nicer to convicted criminals. But this is private school, so there's nobody to complain to except my dad.

Dad got really into the idea of private school when the lead singer for Ribbon Purge told him this really detailed story about how she got beaten up in the bathroom of her public high school and nobody cared, and that's why — Dad figures — she's now in a death metal band and has a really big ring through the center of her nose. He even prepaid my tuition right through graduation, using the rest of the money he inherited when my grandmother died. So there was no getting out of this.

After I ditched the books, I found myself waiting for Bailey again, only this time in the parking lot. Finally I spotted her, walking with a couple of juniors from the lacrosse team. What is it about Bailey that makes her so un-invisible? I wondered, not for the first time. Was it her thick, straight, shiny, strawberry-blond hair? Was it her perfect teeth, long legs, or just the confidence that possession of all these assets had bred in her?

Suddenly, Morgan Logenstern was standing right in front of me, so close I could see the pores on his nose.

"Um, Alex?" he began. I started to shake my head no, then realized that Morgan had Mr. Rosso with me last year, so he probably thought my name *was* Alex.

"It's Xandra, actually." I'm not sure I could have sounded less encouraging, but ol' Morgan seemed unfazed.

"Oh, okay. Anyway, I was just wondering if you had a date for the prom yet?"

Morgan was always one of the smartest people in our class; I guess he'd noticed that just about everybody else in the entire junior class had already paired up.

"I'm actually going to be out of town that weekend," I heard myself telling him.

He sort of nodded and shuffled off. I tried to feel bad for him, but I really just felt bad for me. Now, if by some miracle someone else did ask me to the prom, I couldn't even go.

Bailey reappeared in front of me. "What did that guy want?"

"Just the time," I told her. It was all too pathetic to even bother repeating.

Four hours and thirty-three dresses later, I made it back to Plan A: my apartment, *The Vampire Diaries* on DVR, and

Chinese takeout from Lo Pei down the block. It was a good plan. Dad was at Crash Mansion, DJing some kind of party. Usually he was home on Friday nights. On Sunday nights, he had his weekly radio show followed by his regular DJ gig at Crash, Sunday Night Synth.

I loved my dad's radio show. When I was younger, I would go into the studio with him, although I could never stay awake until midnight when the show ended. I'd sleep in the corner of the studio on an old blanket he kept there just for me. When I got older, I had my own booth at Crash, where I would sit and do homework by fake candlelight, listening to my dad DJ and turning down the middle-aged eighties music fans who approached me. There weren't many — the regulars knew who I was, and the bouncers usually scared the rest away, but some guys don't pick up on your standard social cues. These social cue–impaired guys are still the only ones who ever ask me out.

Thanks to Gavin, I grew up learning every minute detail about retro-progressive music made between about 1978 and 1990 and everything about synthpop made, well, ever. But Gavin kept up with the current music trends, too, as part of his job as program manager at the station.

I think my dad worries about me being too much into his deal, though. Besides Eli, and now Bailey, I don't really have anybody else. Sometimes I like it. Other times, I just want somebody to see me.

But I can entertain myself. Gavin says I've always been good at that. Even when I was really little, I could figure out some way to pass the time on my own. And I still can. I don't even attempt to actually understand my homework in algebra or chem anymore; I just write something down and hand it in, so I have a lot of time to kill. Even more, since Eli and Bailey started dating, and now the plans I would have had on Friday night and Saturday night are *their* plans. Weeknights I still get to hang with them usually. Yay for me.

So the soundtrack in my head right now is full of downtempo music: weird, sad little songs by The Decemberists and Iron & Wine. I just made an actual playlist out of my mental playlist and loaded it onto my iPod. I plugged in my speakers and listened while I cleaned up the apartment, and Thom Yorke's "Black Swan" started playing. It takes a long time to make the perfect playlist. I don't believe in that little Genius button they have on iTunes. That's cheating.

After the place was clean and the Chinese leftovers packed away for Gavin, who still wouldn't be home for hours, I sat on the fire escape and listened, with my headphones in, to the rest of my playlist. I brought my beat-up old tarot deck with me and started doing a spread for myself. The card in the current-situation spot came up the Hanged Man. I didn't really need a portal to the supernatural to know I was stuck — thanks a lot. I wondered what would happen to change things, or if I'd ever get unstuck.

The immediate future card was a new one: the Three of Swords. Not a good card, I knew that much. The picture is just what you'd expect from the name: a big red heart pierced through with three sharp swords. But I couldn't remember if it meant heartbreak or something worse. I thought about looking it up, but I decided to just let my heart-stabbed future remain a mystery. I reshuffled the rest of the cards back into the deck and watched the lights of the city for a long time.

CHAPTER FIVE

WHAT'S YOUR NAME? THAT'S AN EASY QUESTION, RIGHT? IT IS UNLESS YOU'RE ME, APPARENTLY

"I was lost then and I'm lost now
And I doubt I'll ever know which way to go"
— BROKEN BELLS, "VAPORIZE"

Tavares, Florida — Saturday, October 9

I dreamed about elephants, a parade of them, as if the one elephant I'd seen the day before had multiplied like those strings of paper cutout dolls. They kept marching past me, no end in sight. For some reason, in the dream I tried to catch up to each one and hurl myself on its back, but they were moving too fast, their backs were slippery, and I kept falling. Lina, the trapeze girl I'd seen, laughed at me. The long yellow feathers on her hat swayed as she laughed.

"Wake up, new girl!" I heard a voice say.

I wasn't fully awake yet, but on some level I processed that *new girl* was me.

"Awake," I managed to mumble back. I opened one eye and then the other. Doug, the Michael Jackson wannabe, was staring at me.

"Big day — opening night!" he told me. In my groggy state I closed both eyes again. Was he trying to say it was already night again?

"Okay, just lie there, but if you don't get up soon, it's gonna be the bucket for you."

I opened just one eye again. "Bucket?"

"Bucket. As in cold water. Trust me, it's better to just get up."

"I'm up!" I practically shouted as I catapulted out of the compartment. "No bucket! But I have a question. Is there breakfast first? What day is today?"

"It's Saturday. And yes, three squares a day at the cookhouse."

"Good. Because I haven't eaten since . . . um, Thursday? Unless you count the granola bar I had yesterday morning. I think."

Doug's eyes widened. "Damn, girl. Miracle you didn't die last night working so hard on an empty stomach."

"Maybe I did die," I said, looking into the little mirror someone had put up in the "hallway" of the trailer, and sighing before trying to put my hair into a less horrifying ponytail. "That would make this hell, probably."

"Come on, it's not *that* bad. Everything will look better with some bacon and sausage."

"You're quite the carnivore, Doug. I really respect that."

He was already heading out of the trailer. "Nah, I'm just here for the money," he said. "Not really from circus folk."

"I'll try to remember that," I said, and followed him out.

A mess tent had been added to the circus city during the short hours I'd slept, and the kitchen was definitely open. I got in line with Doug and the other members of the crew I'd met last night. It was a lot like a high school cafeteria — at least the ones I'd seen in movies and stuff. The cafeteria at Sheldon did not have trays or milk cartons (but they did have a sashimi bar).

Here at the circus there was a giant pile of trays and a couple of women in aprons serving up what each person asked for. I closed my eyes for a moment and inhaled the scent of bacon, eggs, and biscuits. A hot meal was going to be heaven. And I didn't even have to feel the least bit guilty. I'd definitely earned my keep last night.

I sat with the crew at a table in the back. Just like probably every high school cafeteria, there were clearly cliques. I saw the trapeze girl sitting with a blond girl who also looked like a dancer, and a blond guy who looked exactly like her, who I figured had to be her brother. At the same table I saw a woman who had been working with the elephant the night before, and Louie, the ponytailed man who'd taken pity on me yesterday.

At another table I spotted two clowns; neither one was wearing face makeup, but one wore a shabby old-fashioned suit with a huge tie, and the other wore a striped lime green and yellow suit. I saw Carl, the tent master, sitting with them.

"So it's pretty segregated here, huh?" I asked Heather, who had sat down beside me. She was wearing a massive hoodie and cargo pants. Heather seemed to have an easy time fitting in with the guys on the crew. She was one of those girls you would never buy scented bath stuff for. She was making her way through a massive plate of biscuits.

"You mean how people sit in here?" she asked. "Guess so. Crew people keep with crew, performers with each other. Some performers make their own meals — most of their rigs have pretty decent kitchens. But Carol's food is so good, most everybody eats here. And it's not like you can't talk to anyone else or nothing, just sort of the way we end up sitting. Were you hoping to make it into the show or something? A lot of people come in hoping to perform and end up just . . . working."

"Me — no! I mean, I don't have any talent. I actually just came here looking for my mother." The rest of the table was pretty quiet right at that moment, so I raised my voice. "I wonder if anybody worked with my mother here — it would have been six months ago or so. Callie is her name."

Blank looks greeted me. Joe, the man who'd been nice to me the night before, spoke from the other end of the table. "She weren't with the crew. I been here fifteen seasons. Sorry."

"It's okay," I told him. Well, that was one group down. I really hadn't pictured my mother in with this crew, but still.

"Who's the new girl?" A guy popped up between Heather and me. She swatted at him as he grabbed one of the biscuits off her plate. But then she smiled at him and slid down the bench so that he would fit in between us.

I looked at him as he sat down and ate his biscuit in two big bites. He was gorgeous: blond, tan, with major arm muscles bulging beneath the sleeves of his white T-shirt. He was easily cuter than the cutest guy at Sheldon.

"We're still calling her new girl, actually," Heather told him. "Waiting to see if she bolts before we name her."

"She prob'ly already *has* a name, Heather. Geesh. Ring crew's got such rotten manners. I'm Jamie," he told me, wiping biscuit crumbs off his hand before offering it to me. "I work on the midway — rides, mostly. We are *much* friendlier. And what's your name?"

I stared at him, my mind suddenly a blank. I have this problem talking to cute boys, because I can't. A few too many seconds went by before I forced myself to answer.

"I guess I'm Lexi," I finally managed. "I mean, I used to go by Xandra, because my name's Alexandra," I hurried to explain. "Xandra, Lexi — both of them are nicknames. I just . . . I guess I'm just tired of being Xandra."

"What's so wrong with Xandra?" Jamie asked, stealing another biscuit from Heather.

"Such a good question," Heather said, rolling her eyes.

Jamie laughed at Heather's comment, but then he smiled at me and winked to soften the blow. Then he stood up and went to the food line. I tried not to watch him go or notice his muscles. When he returned with a plate piled high, Heather had already finished and wandered off. Since Doug and most of the other guys were still at the table drinking coffee, though, I stayed where I was. Jamie took Heather's spot and set to work on the food, but after a minute or so, he took a little break to smile at me. "So, Lexi, where are you from?"

"Um, New York. City, I mean."

Here we go again. Usually, I can talk like a perfectly normal person. I mean, sometimes I use a few too many big words, but that's just because I have more books than friends. But I can use, you know, complete sentences. Unless there's a boy involved.

"New York City." Jamie whistled like he was impressed, and also like he hadn't noticed he was talking to a moron. "I've never been. Always wanted to go. So, big-city girl, huh? What are you doing here?"

"I . . . well . . . I didn't have anywhere else to go."

Jamie nodded. "Sounds about right. That's a lot of people here, anyhow. Outsiders — people from the real world. Sometimes people come for a job thinking it's glamorous, or they're writing an article or a book. But mostly they're just running."

"So your family worked in the circus?" I asked him. "Did you travel around when you were, like, little?"

"Yep. Fourth generation. It's not so bad. For one, I didn't have to go to school."

I tried not to show my surprise on my face. In spite of my cell-block schedule this year, I'd never, not once, considered not finishing school. What would a person do without even a high school degree? I guess he would kind of have to keep doing what he was doing now.

Jamie didn't seem to be worried about his lack of education; he was fully focused on consuming mass quantities of breakfast. He kept making small talk around the chewing, asking me about New York and why I'd joined the ring crew. I told him that I had begged Louie for any job. I looked around the table, startled to find Doug and the rest of the guys had disappeared.

"Oh!" I said, mostly to myself, but Jamie was close enough to hear.

"Whatsit?" he asked, his mouth full of sausage and gravy.

"The rest of the crew just left — and I don't know where they went. Or where I'm supposed to go." I was embarrassed to have stopped paying attention. I did *not* want to have to bother Louie again.

But Jamie promptly did that for me. "Yo! Louie!" he yelled, and everyone at Louie's table turned to stare at me. I felt my cheeks go red. "What you got on tap for Lexi today?"

"I'm sure he just wants me to go find Joe and do whatever he says," I whispered to Jamie, trying not to move my mouth too much.

"Nah, that was load-in day. You're not big enough to be crew," Jamie told me in his normal — loud — voice.

"Novelties wagon tonight," Louie said to Jamie. He didn't seem to notice that I'd introduced myself to him with a different name. It probably didn't matter what I called myself, as long as I showed up to work. "Angela went back to California after the last stop. Tell Heather to get her started."

"That won't take all day," Jamie told him, taking a huge swig of coffee.

"Then she can watch the rehearsal today," Louie said, a hint of something that looked almost like a smile creeping in. "She won't get another chance to see the circus, eh? Lina, you will show her a good seat, yes?" He turned to his daughter, the pretty but frosty trapeze girl from the night before. She smiled at him but gave me a dark look.

"Great," I said under my breath. "Thank you!" I said much louder to Louie. "And thank you, too," I said, turning to Jamie.

He was already gathering up his tray. "No sweat, new girl. Enjoy the circus."

I looked over at Lina, who was still looking at me. I couldn't read her expression, but I knew it wasn't excitement about babysitting me.

"Great," I muttered again. I would rather have rejoined the ring crew. But at least my stomach was full.

I sat uncomfortably until Lina finished her tiny breakfast, then followed her out. I followed her into the big tent and sat where she pointed.

The ring was empty and silent when I took my seat. I waited for the show to start.

CHAPTER SIX

ADVENTURE BARBIE

"Life in plastic, it's fantastic"
— AQUA, "BARBIE GIRL"

13 Broome Street—Friday, May 21

There are a lot of reasons why everyone in the known universe has a boyfriend except for me. I can list the top five on command, just in case anyone's ever interested. No one ever has been, but that's no reason not to be prepared.

Number five: I blame my parents. They were ridiculously all over each other in a lovey-dovey, make-you-want-to-barf way. I'm talking goo-goo eyes and hand-holding. That is, until one day my mom up and left and I learned really quickly not to even mention her name. So that's one reason to actively choose to be single.

Four: Everyone at my school, I'm pretty sure, paired up in the eighth grade. Occasionally they'd switch partners, as though there were some secret game of musical chairs being played somewhere in the back hallway. But there was never any warning, and no one was ever single for more than a few minutes. Got to keep butts in those seats.

Reason number three: I always have something sarcastic to say. That one is probably self-explanatory.

Two: I'm antisocial. Unless it's a concert, I have a hard time making myself get all dolled up to go out, coughing up fifteen bucks' cover charge, and holding the same plastic cup of soda for five hours because drinks are twelve bucks a pop.

And finally, reason number one: Adventure Barbie.

When girls like me, who are relatively smart and pretty, who have something to say, and who have their own points of view, spend every Friday night home alone watching reality TV, this is because all of the guys they might potentially have dated are out with Adventure Barbie.

You know who she is — that girl with the perfectly tousled hair, long legs, and no fat anywhere because she doesn't eat. She wears super-high heels, which she can walk in perfectly, but she also comes equipped with hiking boots. A guy who finds himself an A.B. is pleased to find out that she is equally at home zip-lining and fine dining. She will go with him to his kickboxing gym and impress all the guys there, and then she will go home and change into a little black dress and five-inch heels. A.B. does not exist in nature; she is her own creation. And no regular girl can match her. A regular girl's face betrays her panic when she is asked to go rock climbing or cliff diving. A regular girl looks like a drowned rat after an afternoon of white-water rafting. But not Adventure Barbie.

The ways of the A.B. are very mysterious, though. I should know: I have been friends with one for going on three years now. But Bailey and her skills remain a mystery to me. I watched her perform her magic on all the cutest upperclassmen — briefly upsetting their incestuous game of musical chairs — before, for some reason, she picked Eli. And it was too much to hope that Eli would be immune to the charms of Adventure Barbie. They went skydiving for his birthday last month. Adorable.

It was another (dateless) Friday afternoon, and I stood outside the art room waiting for Eli. I figured walking home from school would be the only time I'd see him until Bailey let him up for air somewhere around the middle of Sunday. I didn't know what they had planned for this weekend; I only knew they'd look like a page from the Abercrombie & Fitch catalog doing it. Bailey had performed quite the makeover on Eli.

"Hey, X. What are you doing here?" Eli had finally emerged from the art room.

"Bird-watching." I gave him a dirty look.

Eli looked confused. Maybe all the dye from his stylish new clothes had affected his brain cells.

"Duh, I'm waiting for you. I kinda thought that was obvious," I told him.

"I thought you'd be halfway home by now." When I didn't say anything, he rushed to add, "I know how much you hate this place."

"You used to hate it, too," I muttered, turning away from him and starting back down the hall.

I didn't get far; Eli held on to one of the straps of my

backpack. "Wait up, Xan. I'm sorry. I mean, I don't know what I did, but whatever it is, I'm sorry about it."

"That is the lamest apology in the history of the world." I shrugged out of my backpack straps so that he would let go, but he didn't. "Seriously, Eli, whatever — later." I turned away again.

Eli let go of my backpack, but then he surprised me by grabbing my waist and pulling me toward him. "X . . . I'm sorry for everything — just all of it," he said softly in my ear; he was standing very close to me, one hand still on my waist.

I swallowed hard, trying to ignore the stupid, useless feelings that his hand on my waist was causing. I wanted to either take one step closer and lay my head on his chest or run away. Everything in between just seemed too horrible to contemplate. I made myself count to ten so he wouldn't see how much I wanted to get away from him. When I got to ten I stepped back, forced myself to laugh it all off. "Eli, chillax. I'm just getting sick or something. It's making me cranky — ignore me. I'll see you Sunday, yeah?"

Eli looked down at me for a second before agreeing. "Yeah, sure. Sunday. Bails and I are going to go hiking tomorrow — at her dad's place in Tarrytown."

"Of course you are," I muttered, turning away and really making my escape this time.

"See you Sunday!" I heard him call out behind me. His voice already sounded far away.

CHAPTER SEVEN

CIRCUS SCHOOL

"There's only two types of people in the world
The ones that entertain and the ones that observe"
— BRITNEY SPEARS, "CIRCUS"

Tavares, Florida — Saturday, October 9

A clown on stilts led the parade. The performers came out
into the ring two at a time, in bright and sparkly costumes,
to the sound of old-fashioned circus music. They were waving and smiling, but at the moment I was the only person
actually sitting in any of the seats, until I saw Louie lead a
small group toward some seats across the ring from me. It
seemed like a strange crowd for the circus. It was mostly men
in suits and a lady who looked just like one of the librarians
from Sheldon.

When I looked back at the ring, I recognized some
of the animal handlers, now all in costumes. I even spotted
the grumpy tiger man wearing a tiger-striped suit and
a top hat. The performers took their places in the ring
in three long lines. They put their heads down, waiting,
and then the beat of the music changed, and they began

doing their choreography, dancing to Katy Perry's "Firework." Some of them — I spotted Lina's long, elegant frame right away — were amazing dancers. The animal trainers knew the steps but were clearly clumsier.

It would have been nice to watch with someone, I thought glumly as I sat alone. But I was getting used to being alone. It wasn't that different from my old life. Wait — yes, it was! I hadn't really been alone then — I'd had a family. But sitting here and crying was not an option I was going to allow myself, so I pressed both hands to my eyes and willed the tears back.

"I've seen better, but the charivari's not that bad," came a voice from somewhere under my left arm. I opened my eyes and saw Jamie sitting beside me, his head down to talk to me in my hunched-over position.

"Hi," I said, redoubling my not-crying effort. "What's a charivari?" I managed. New vocabulary was always a safe bet, emotionally speaking. I always liked learning words.

He chuckled. "Never been to the circus before?" he asked. "It's the opening part of the show. It used to be just the clowns in the old days, but now most shows have a musical number with the whole cast."

"Oh," I said. "I haven't actually been to the circus before," I added. "There's one in the city — the Big Apple Circus? But I've never been."

Jamie whistled through his teeth. "Yeah, that's a big

show. Probably the best one. They have a lot of sponsors, get a lot of press. Even did that Britney Spears video a couple years ago. We're a little smaller. They don't change our show up year to year. Last year, Louie got this idea that he was going to try and hire this director guy from Chicago and all. But that did *not* go well — he fired him, like, two days later. Louie likes being the one in charge."

I smiled, picturing someone trying to direct Louie — I could already see where that might be a problem. Although at that moment, Louie was sort of fawning over one of the men he'd brought in with him.

"Who's that old guy over there?" I asked Jamie.

"Good call — he's actually our major sponsor. Lives around here, somewhere. He's got, like, four private planes, supposedly. He likes the show — went to the circus in England when he was a little kid, so he sponsors it every year. Louie has to really kiss up to him."

"I would have thought the circus was sort of profitable on its own," I whispered. The two clowns from breakfast weren't sticking to the choreography, and one of them had a little dog. They kept messing up and getting in the way. I saw the old airplane guy laugh.

"Not so much," Jamie said. "The animals are incredibly expensive. But it wouldn't really be a circus without them."

The dance number ended, and Louie left his seat and walked out to announce the first act. He was in full ringleader costume: top hat, red coat and tails with a line of gold sequins on each lapel, black shirt, black pants, and tall boots.

He addressed the money guy directly and bowed in his direction a couple of times.

First up was a woman I recognized as the elephant handler; she wore a spangly red, white, and blue costume — complete with sequined patriotic-colored hat — and she led the elephant out into the ring. She was holding a big metal cylinder in one hand and a whip in the other.

"That's Marina," Jamie whispered. "She's really good. She's, like, sixth-generation circus, all animal people."

I turned to him. "How come you're not in the show? Didn't you say you were, like, fifth generation or something?"

"Fourth, far as I know," he corrected me. "Like I said, not much money in it. Someday there won't be any more Bobs — the sponsor guy," he added at my look of confusion. "Old dudes who loved the circus when they were kids. But the carnival part, that's here to stay. And I was never much of a show-business guy. I like machines, so I work the midway. That's where all the action is, anyway. Only the little kids come to see the show. The rest of the town turns out after for the rides, the games, the food."

"Makes sense," I told him as Marina led the elephant to sit, then stand on the pedestal she'd brought in. Then the elephant got down low, and Marina got up on his back and rode around the ring. I had a disturbing flashback to my dream. "Nice elephant," I said.

"Bull," Jamie said. "They call them bulls when they're in the show. The next part's my favorite. Julian's the fire-eater. Now that's a righteous gig."

I suppressed a giggle at Jamie's choice of words. I watched as Marina rode her elephant — bull — out of the ring. Then a wiry man in a slightly shabby tux walked into the middle of the ring. He began a complex pantomime, but there was no fire anywhere. I turned to Jamie to ask what was going on.

"I guess he's not gonna do it for rehearsal." Jamie shook his head. "Shame. Julian's getting up there in years. And he had a close call last season. Guess they're playing it safe." The little man bowed, doffing his bowler hat to reveal slicked-down jet-black hair. He turned to Jamie and me after he'd bowed to the money guy and bowed to us. I thought I saw him wink.

I realized I was actually having fun, sitting here watching the show with Jamie. The cute-boy effect had largely worn off. I'd even been speaking in full, coherent sentences for the last half hour. We watched the comedy act — the two clowns back with the dog. Jamie told me that they always brought a little kid in as part of their act, and it was really sweet. Although they had to be careful selecting the kid, he said. Sometimes they picked one who just sort of froze, and then it was awkward. I figured I would have been the kid to freeze.

Next came a wire act. "That's Faina," Jamie said, pointing to a whip-thin girl with pale skin and very pale blond hair. "She's, like, seventh generation — further back than anybody except the Vranas. And all wire and trapeze people. She was probably born in midair." He smiled.

"A little crush on wire girl?" I asked him. He was certainly regarding her more intently than he had the clowns.

He grinned. "Once, maybe. We went out when we were both younger. But now her husband would crush me to powder. She married a guy from Ringling. They hardly ever even see each other, but it seems to suit Faina just fine. Besides, Faina is . . . Well, let's just say, nothing ever really pleases Faina. She drives Louie insane."

She was very graceful on the wire, moving slowly in time with avant-garde-sounding music. Her act was cool, but the weird music kind of ruined it for me. Faina dismounted, bowed — this time only to Bob, ignoring Jamie and me — and ran off. The next act was two tigers that jumped through a big hoop that Jamie said would be on fire for the actual show. Then Jamie said, "And here's the finale."

Lina entered, along with the other elegant girl from breakfast and the guy who looked just like her. The two girls stood on one side on a platform, and the boy was on the other. They were all wearing black leotards, but not fancy costumes. The girls' hair was pulled back tight. They had similar faces — angular, with high cheekbones and aristocratic features. But Lina had very dark hair, and the other girl was fair-skinned and her hair was dark blond.

"That's Lina, Eliska, and Edvar." Jamie snorted. "But he goes by Eddie, for obvious reasons. They're all Louie's kids, of course."

"Not your favorite person, Eddie?"

"He's a pain, but whatever. The girls are okay. Lina's awesome. Eliska is kind of frosty until you get to know her."

"If Lina's warm compared to her sister, then I need to steer clear," I said before I had time to stop myself. "Sorry — it's nothing. Louie gave me a job; his kids can be whatever temperature they want. I'll shut up now."

"Don't need to on my account," Jamie said. "You came on as crew, so none of them probably even noticed you. They're a nice family, though."

"I thought Eddie was a pain?"

"Well, yeah, except him."

There were a couple of guys from the ring crew checking the nets that were rigged beneath the swings of the trapeze. Lina looked massively annoyed.

"Jamie, will you please make yourself useful and check the rigging?" she called down to him.

Jamie smiled sheepishly at me before leaping away to do her bidding. "No problem, Lina."

He checked things out for a couple of minutes, then gave Lina the thumbs-up, and she called "Ready" across to her brother.

"Eddie's the catcher," Jamie said, back beside me. "Lina's doing a regular catch and return to warm up now. Then the first move's an angel — the catcher will hold her by the feet and one arm."

"You seem to know a lot about this," I told him. "And she had you check the net or whatever."

He looked sheepish again. "Yeah, my family's done trapeze forever. My mom was a flyer. But look at me — too big."

I looked him over. I wouldn't say his size was any sort of problem, but looking up at Eddie flying in midair, I realized he kind of had a point. "Are you sad about it?"

"Not even a little," Jamie said. "It's a pretty harsh life. Lots of injuries, and you have to be really careful what you eat. No thanks."

I remembered Jamie's unrestrained bacon festival that morning at breakfast and smiled. "I'm with you. I don't plan to give up bacon and French fries until it's under doctor's orders."

"My kind of girl." Jamie winked at me, and I blushed.

We both looked up and watched Lina's sister do a knee hang from the trapeze. My breath caught at the sight, but she easily swung over to where Eddie caught her. I looked across the ring; Bob's attention was rapt. "I can see why this is the finale," I said.

"Yeah, it's pretty awesome," Jamie said. "But it's no Hurricane." He smiled. "My ride."

"I know the Hurricane!" I told him. There was one on the boardwalk in New Jersey — Sea Isle, if I remembered right. I had ridden it once with Eli and my dad when we were younger.

"I'd say you should come ride it tonight," he told me, "but apparently you're gonna be busy selling stuffed tigers and cotton candy in the novelties wagon."

"I guess that's the plan," I said. It definitely sounded better than being Costi's assistant, so I wasn't about to complain.

Lina, Eliska, and Eddie soared through the air a few more times, doing some flips. Eddie could do a triple, Jamie informed me — flipping around three times in midair before catching the bar again. I heard a gasp and was surprised when it turned out it came from me.

"Yeah. He's really good," Jamie said, not sounding too pleased about it.

And then it was over, and I was blinking in the bright sunlight outside the tent. "Thanks for watching with me," I said to Jamie, meaning it. "It was cool to listen to a circus expert."

"No problemo," he said. "Hey, I gotta go check on some things over on the midway. You'll be okay?"

I had no idea where I was supposed to go, or what I was supposed to do, but I nodded, not wanting to keep him. I saw Louie heading out of the tent, and I figured I'd risk annoying him and ask. Better to ask for a job than to have him think I was lazy, right?

I took a step back, squinting up at the outside of the tent. I saw the name *Circus Europa* in white script letters on the side. I realized I must not have been on the name side of the tent the night before.

"Is it named after the woman from mythology, with Zeus and the white bull?" I turned to Jamie, but noticed that Louie was standing beside him, head cocked to one side.

"In a roundabout way," Louie answered. "My great-great-grandfather named it so. He broke away from his father's show, which was called Jupiter —"

"Oh, I get it! Europa's one of Jupiter's moons. They are all named for Zeus's — Jupiter's — lovers. Clever."

"Yes, I would say so." Louie nodded, regarding me thoughtfully. "The story has been passed down through the family. Most people simply think the name refers to the style of the show — a one-ring show in the European style."

"Like Big Apple," I said, remembering my conversation with Jamie. "I think I read in the *New York Post* that it was the same kind of show."

Louie nodded again, looking at me in what seemed to be an appraising way. "You read a lot, do you?"

I nodded. "Yes." I didn't tell him that I often read stupid Regency novels.

"You are finished with school?"

"No, sir. I am — was — a senior. I've got a semester and a half to go. In high school," I added, when he still looked confused.

"I have another job for you," he told me. "The teacher, she left before the last stop. I sent for another, but she won't be here for a few days. You teach, yes?"

"Teach what? I mean, who would I be teaching?"

"We've got circus school," Jamie told me. He'd been hovering.

"I thought you said you didn't go to school."

He shook his head, and I saw Louie shoot him some sort

of look. "I didn't grow up on *this* show," Jamie said. "Louie woulda made me go to school. All the kids here go. There aren't that many. Maybe six?"

"Eight when they all show up," Louie said. "Jamie will show you where. You can do this?"

I felt myself nodding. "I can try. I mean, as long as you know I'm still technically a student myself."

"Better than nothing," Louie said, and turned heel and walked away.

"And with that stunning endorsement," I said, then looked at Jamie. "What's bothering you?" I asked him. He was looking up at the tent, and he looked confused.

"Nothing." He turned and motioned for me to follow him — presumably taking me to my new gig at circus school. He shook his head. "I just thought it was named after Europe," I heard him say, and I stifled a giggle as I followed him down the midway.

Circus school turned out to be in a nice trailer, smaller than the one the crew slept in, but bigger than the ones the performers slept in. Along the walls were low bookshelves, a couple of computers, and a little refrigerator. There was even a shelf of toys and a very small plastic shelf of games. There were six kids inside. The smallest looked like a first or second grader, maybe. He was sitting on the floor playing with some space-robot-type action figures. The oldest was sitting curled up in a chair, reading. She was definitely close to my age, and I'd seen her before. In fact, I'd just seen her about a half hour before, only then she'd been in a black leotard, flying through the air. It was Louie's other daughter, Eliska. Her hair was still in a bun, and she wore heavy stage makeup, but she was dressed in jeans and a hoodie now.

Jamie seemed to have been right about the sisters; Eliska shot me a look that made Lina's regard seem almost friendly.

Jamie had brought me to the trailer, and he addressed the older woman sitting on the floor surrounded by the three younger kids. "Maggie, Louie sent Lexi here to fill in for today. Sounds like the new teacher's gonna be here in the next couple days." He turned back to me and said, "Maggie's been filling in since we left Georgia."

"Hi," I said, wondering silently why Maggie didn't just keep filling in. She was obviously at least out of school, unlike me.

Maggie smiled, revealing some missing teeth. "Hi yourself. I'll be glad to get back to me lads," she added. She wasted no time in patting the little ones on their heads and hightailing it out of the trailer. I didn't even have time to ask who or what the lads were.

Jamie looked a bit uncomfortable. "Okay, so you're fine here? Eliska can tell you where everybody left off. See you later."

Awesome. Eliska had gone back to her book. I decided at that point I didn't have anything to lose. My community service of choice back at Sheldon had always been reading to the kids at the library near my apartment, so I figured that was a safe start.

"Hey, everybody," I said to the kids on the floor. A boy and girl who both looked about fourteen sat apart, each at a computer playing solitaire. I figured I had better get the munchkins squared away first, and then maybe tackle the older ones. "Anybody ever play the Animal Name Game?" I always used that at the library — little kids like animals, and they like to tell you their names.

One little boy immediately started yelling "Jimmy Jaguar! Jimmy Jaguar!" at the top of his lungs.

"I guess that's one yes." I smiled at him. "Okay, so you're all set," I said to Jimmy. "And I'm Lexi. What animal should I be?" I asked them.

"Lion!" a little girl with red hair yelled. The boy over at the computer said, "Lemur."

"I could be a liger," I said to be diplomatic. "A mix of a lion and a tiger."

"Cool!" said Jimmy Jaguar. We went around the circle and hashed out choices. The little red-haired boy was named Connor, but he wanted to be a dinosaur, and none of us could think of any dinosaurs whose names started with a C. I finally just let him be Connor Tyrannosaurus Rex just to make him happy.

Eliska kept her nose in her book, but the computer twins both politely picked animals to go with their names. I asked them where to find some books — Connor T-Rex was starting to make siren noises, so I figured I'd better hurry. We found some picture books, and I breathed a sigh of relief when I found one I knew: *The Stinky Cheese Man and Other Fairly Stupid Tales*. I read it to them, using funny voices for different characters in the story. I made Chicken Licken have a Cockney accent, and this particularly tickled Jimmy. And once one kid that age starts laughing, the rest pretty much join in. Then when we were done reading, I had them help me find paper and markers, and I told them to draw their favorite character from the stories. Connor drew me as a pink Stegosaurus with long brown hair.

Once they were all happily coloring, I faced the only real lion in the room, Eliska, in her den. "So Jamie said you could tell me where you left off?" I asked her. I kept my voice neutral, like she could answer me or not, I didn't care.

"How old are you?" she asked me instead.

"Seventeen. I'm a senior."

"Me as well. I am a senior. Why would Louie send you to teach me?" Her tone was not neutral. It was snotty.

I just looked at her, biting back words. I wanted to tell her, *Yeah, you're a senior in this* trailer, *and I have one semester to go at one of the top prep schools in Manhattan.* (For once I forgot how I hated the whole prep-school superiority thing.) And I also really wanted to point out that if she was so educated, she could have been helping the younger ones, instead of sitting in the corner like a waste. But I didn't say either of those things. Thank God. Instead, I decided to ignore her. I turned to Annabelle and John, the two older kids by the computers. "Is there something you guys were working on that I could maybe help you with?" I asked them.

John didn't seem inclined to do much except play on the computer, but he and Annabelle were both more polite than Eliska — not that it would take much — and they got up and led me to the bookshelves.

"With our old teacher we mostly did these math packets," Annabelle said, holding up an outdated-looking workbook. "But I don't really want to work on those."

"Ew, I don't blame you," I told her. "I don't really understand math, either. I guess we could pick out a book to read," I told them, stalling. Other than reading to kids like I had done at the library, I had zero ideas.

"I liked those funny voices," John said, almost shyly. "I mean, when you read before."

"Thanks," I said, surprised. "I like doing different kinds of accents. My friend El — well, my old best friend back home and I used to pick an accent and talk in it for the rest of the day."

"I bet that's funny," Annabelle said.

I answered in my fake French accent, "Eet eez, Annabelle, eet totally eez," and she giggled.

I spotted a copy of *To Kill a Mockingbird* on the shelf and went over to grab it. "Either of you guys ever read this?"

They both shook their heads no. I saw Eliska watching me over the edge of her AP Lit exam review book, but I tried to ignore her. "Well, you have to — read it, I mean. It's just one of those books that everybody needs to read someday.

Want me to read a little to you? I mean, we have to do something, right?"

John looked kind of doubtful. I wondered how many days he'd already spent doing nothing in this trailer.

"I could do an accent . . ." Once I'd talked like Scout for an entire twenty-four hours. Gavin had had to —

I stopped myself from remembering and concentrated on the kids. I opened the book and started reading, figuring they could listen or not.

"When he was nearly thirteen, my brother Jem got his arm badly broken at the elbow," I started in my best Alabama twang.

They both listened as I read the first three chapters, and then Maggie came back to take them all to lunch.

Eliska didn't follow the others, so it was just the two of us sitting there in awkward silence. For some reason, it seemed important to me not to be the first one to leave, so I started tidying up the books. Then I started alphabetizing them. Finally, Eliska closed her book, stood up, looked at me, and said, "You're better than the last teacher we had." She didn't wait for a response, just turned and walked out of the trailer.

After school, I went back to my compartment in the trailer. My bag was sitting on the bunk, waiting for me. I sat down beside it and rooted around until I found the tarot deck I'd brought with me. I pulled out the cards, shuffled the deck, closed my eyes, and chose one card. I wasn't even sure of the question I was asking — I guess I just wanted to know if everything was going to work out all right. I flipped over the Tower: catastrophe, turmoil, and upheaval. I jammed the card back into the pile and shoved them all back in the box. Then I pushed the bag to the end of the compartment and curled up to try to take a nap. It seemed like only seconds had passed before Heather appeared beside me.

It was time for my second job of the day: cashier girl at the novelties wagon.

Heather led me to the "wagon" in question: a rectangle-shaped trailer painted to look like an old-fashioned train caboose. A big flap on one side was open so that customers could see inside. The pegboard on the walls was covered with neat rows of little stuffed lions, tigers, and elephants, premade bags of cotton candy, and streamers with *Circus Europa* written in white on red ribbon attached to little sticks. The wooden counter held a small cash register, a stack of souvenir programs, and a whole bunch of glow-stick novelties in clear plastic bins.

Heather spent about a minute showing me where everything was and how to work the register. Then she was gone, and before I knew it, I was peering down at an adorable little boy who was pointing excitedly up at the lions.

"How much are the lions?" his dad asked me. It was a good question. I rummaged around the little trailer until for some reason I lifted up the register, and I breathed a sigh of relief to see a price list there.

"Four fifty," I told him. The dad paid, and I watched the little boy do a happy dance when he grabbed his lion.

From the opening in the wagon, I could see the entrance to the ring for the main show. I could also smell things getting started: popcorn, candy apples — there was even a meat-on-a-stick place that made my belly rumble. I realized I'd missed lunch and was about to work through dinner, and sighed. I was just beginning to eye the cotton candy, which I don't even like, when Jamie showed up with a hot dog and a Coke.

"You're not a vegetarian, are you?" he asked with a grin.

I didn't remind him that he'd watched me eat bacon at breakfast. "Nope. And this is the best thing anyone's ever brought me. Literally. I was dying of starvation." I bit into the hot dog, accidentally making a loud *mmm* noise, and I heard Jamie laugh. It was even better than an NYC vendor dog.

"Guess it was a good call," Jamie said as he watched me polish off the dog. "Hey, if they didn't tell you, this wagon's only open before and after both shows. If you wanna come ride the Hurricane later, you can. I'll let you jump the line."

With that he was gone. I could almost hear the thump of the giant Hurricane speakers, all the way at the end of the midway. It was something top forty, a song I almost knew. And then the ring got quiet for a second, and I recognized it. It was the same song I'd heard my last night in New York, standing on the street and wondering where I would go. God, had that been less than a week ago? I'd had four jobs in the last two days alone. But at least I had a place to sleep, food to eat, and people who knew my name. Maybe it was a start.

CHAPTER EIGHT

BUBBLE GIRL DOESN'T GET HER WAFFLES

"Looking at my watch and I'm half past caring"
— THE TRASHCAN SINATRAS, "OBSCURITY KNOCKS"

Seward Park — Sunday, May 23

This book I'm reading is really making me mad.

I'd reread all the Jane Austen novels for about the fortieth time, and the nice little old lady who owns the used bookstore on Leonard Street — she's the one to blame for selling me all those Austen paperbacks in the first place — recommended these Regency books to me. There are just millions of them, all really short, and all romances set around the same time as old Jane. They're awful. I just can't stop reading them.

This one is particularly heinous. Theodora — that's the heroine's name — is just so tiny and beautiful that everyone is so in love with her. Her father, she has him wrapped around her little finger, and she's supposed to marry Captain Randall, and he's off at war, but in the meantime his cousin Lord Tilson is there for some reason (he doesn't seem to have anything better to do), hovering around, and because she's so freaking tiny and beautiful, he's just after her. He wants little Theo for himself. And they go out driving in the park, and Tilson is all over it, his big chance. He always finds a way to touch her — on the knee, under the table; when they dance, he dances too close. (The waltz!) And poor Theo just can't stand it. She's promised to marry the captain, but Tilson just keeps finding opportunities to lay his hands on her. Even though it's totally forbidden.

So that's what's making me mad. Little Theo lives in a repressed society, and this dude just can't stop touching her, and everyone else is always hugging her, dancing with her . . .

Meanwhile, I live in modern-day New York, *downtown*, no less, and it's like I'm a bubble girl. No one holds my hand. The only dancing I ever do is at Crash, and it's to eighties alternative music — all by myself. I guess I take after my dad — Gavin's not really a touchy kind of guy, either. Eli never used to be, until Bailey came along. Now he's a regular old Lord Tilson — with her.

I was actually waiting for the happy couple in the park, and I was trying to read slowly because I only had about forty-five more pages. Since Eli and Bailey are always late now, I was going to be down to people-watching when the pages ran out. I had a hunch that things were going to work out pretty good for Theo. I wished I had as much confidence in my own romantic future. If you didn't count Morgan Logenstern, and I didn't want to, I was in the middle of a pretty impressive dating dry spell, reaching all the way back to a three-date relationship with Robert Marston during sophomore year. I blamed my dad — he had to send me to Sheldon Prep. The guys there — well, I'd actually rather blame them. The alternative is that there's something fundamentally wrong with me.

"Xandra!" Bailey's voice carried across the park, and I looked up from page 204, where I'd been stalled for the past ten minutes, to see her bounding toward me, Eli trailing behind.

"Are you reading *romance* novels again?" I didn't like the way Bailey said *romance*, kind of taunting, and judge-y.

"I have to get my thrills somehow," I told her in my driest voice.

Bailey grabbed the book out of my hands and read the title on the cover. "*The Forbidden Duke*! Oh man, Eli, come here, you *have* to see this."

I snatched the book out of her hands. "Shut up, Bailey." I put the book in my bag.

"Yeah, shut up, Bailey," Eli said, smiling at me. I'd have been grateful for the rescue except I'm pretty sure he'd just missed the entire exchange. "Breakfast?" he asked me.

"You paying?" I asked, illustrating my poverty by pulling the pockets of my jeans inside out and revealing only three bucks and change.

"I gotcha, X," Bailey answered. She had appropriated Eli's nickname for me. Bailey appropriated a lot of things.

"Thanks." I got up and started walking out of the park. I figured Bailey's offer to help subsidize breakfast was an olive branch for the book thing, and I was grateful. I really was pretty cashless, and unlike just about every other kid I knew, I didn't have a debit or a credit card. I knew I'd be spending most of Sunday selling off some of my CDs on Amazon.

"Wait, X." Eli's voice stopped me. "We're going to that diner over on Pike."

"But we always go to Mike's." I stopped walking.

"Bailey says their egg white omelets taste like butt." Eli smiled down at her, pulling her against his side.

"This is what we get for hanging out with people who actually eat egg white omelets," I growled, but rolled my eyes dramatically and smiled to soften the words.

"I know. Bails, before you came along, we were strictly a waffle crowd."

"Some of us are *still* part of the waffle crowd. I figure I have a good ten years until I have to worry about cholesterol."

Bailey reached out her free hand, the one Eli didn't have, and pulled me closer to them. "Cheer up, X. They'll have plenty of cholesterol at the Pike place, I promise. So, anyway, I got tickets . . ."

My ears perked up. Tickets? Bailey's dad did something bank-related — I guess that's why they lived downtown when the family seemed kind of uptown to me. But somehow music was involved.

"Iron & Wine?" she said. "I think I've heard you talk about them."

"Him. And yeah, I have. Ticket for me? Pretty please?"

"Ticket for you." Bailey laughed and turned to Eli. "She

really gets crazy about music. Such a chip off the old Gavin block."

Eli nodded and raised an eyebrow. "You have no idea. We almost got arrested once for trying to sneak backstage to see the Trashcan Sinatras."

"The Trashcan Whos?" Bailey asked.

"Obscure early nineties Irish band. Pretty decent live. Xandra over here just had to get an autograph. Those boys just wanted to get out of there and back on the road. They were pretty rude, actually."

I nodded sadly. "I can't listen to their music the same anymore. It's like a tragedy."

"So we are on for next weekend?" Bailey asked.

"Sure!"

I had cause to regret my enthusiasm a couple of minutes later when we got to the diner. Turns out the tickets were just to soften the blow. Bailey announced at breakfast that she was going to the Hamptons for all of June and most of July to stay at her parents' house there. And Eli was going with her.

And the waffles at the diner on Pike tasted like butt.

CHAPTER NINE

DATING ADVICE FROM THE FIRE-EATER

"And if I was bored, you know I would
And if I was yours, but I'm not"
— ARCADE FIRE, "READY TO START"

Winter Springs, Florida — Sunday, October 17

I was sitting in one of the plastic chairs that someone had set up outside the crew trailer, reading and thinking that it was weird that it was still hot in the middle of October. We had moved sites, and I'd helped again with the setup, already feeling more like I knew the drill. The little circus city sprang up from nothing but empty field once again, right before my eyes.

A shadow fell over *The Desperate Viscount*, and I looked up to see Louie's daughters standing over me.

"You wanna come to town with us?" Lina asked.

Her almost-black hair was down for a change, and it hung to her waist. She was wearing a one-shoulder black top and skinny jeans. Even without makeup, she looked exotically pretty. Her sister, Eliska, stood just behind her. She didn't wear makeup, either, that I could see, but her hair was in a messy bun and she wore a T-shirt and pink cardigan sweater paired with nondescript jeans.

I was so surprised, I almost waited too long to answer, because I saw an expression of annoyance just start to cross Lina's face. But I regained my composure and answered, "Sure!" with probably too much enthusiasm. Lina turned and started walking toward the parking lot, and Eliska followed her. I raced inside the trailer, grabbed my wallet and cell phone, and caught up to them.

"There's a mall about fifteen minutes from here," Lina told me as I came up beside her. "It has a Barnes & Noble, so we thought you'd like to go."

"Thanks for thinking of me," I said, still surprised. "I didn't . . . I mean, just thanks. It will be nice to have a change of scenery for a bit."

Lina rolled her eyes. "Imagine being stuck here all your life. We have to get out sometimes or we'd go crazy."

Lina had led the way to an old gray Honda Civic. It was very clean, especially on the inside. Lina got behind the wheel, and Eliska surprised me by getting in the back. She had an iPhone with her and seemed to be reading a book on it.

"Don't worry about Liska," Lina told me as she put the key in the engine. "She doesn't talk that much."

As we drove down a moderately busy two-lane highway, Lina asked me questions about why I'd come to the circus, where I was from, what New York was like. I skirted around the details, but I did tell her that my father had died and that I'd originally come looking for my mother. "When she wasn't here, I pretty much had to find a job and a place to live," I explained. "And your dad was nice enough to give me a job that came with a place to live."

Lina snorted. "If you want to call it that. Besides, dad's given you jobs, *plural*. And crew quarters — I don't know, I don't feel like you belong there. Especially after what just happened, losing your dad and all."

I didn't argue with Lina. As grateful as I was, I still wasn't really sleeping. Jamie had helped me rig up a little privacy curtain like most of the other crew members had. But I was afraid to sleep, because of the nightmares about my last days in New York. And then there was the fact that the bathroom was a portable job outside the trailer — a fact that had me cursing my small bladder several times a night.

We had come to a stoplight. Lina looked over at me. "I'm real sorry about your dad. And I'm glad you could find some work here." She seemed to be deciding something, and was quiet for a few minutes. We pulled into the parking lot for the mall, the Oviedo Marketplace, and we all piled out of the car.

"Books first," Eliska said, and led the way. Lina just smiled sort of indulgently at her sister, and we followed her into the Barnes & Noble. Lina stopped at the Starbucks counter at the front of the store. "You want anything?"

I looked down at the wallet in my hand and decided that a four-dollar coffee was no longer in the budget. Trying not to sound regretful, I said, "No, I'm okay, thanks."

Lina shot me a look. "My treat. You got my sister to stop complaining about the school for three whole days. That's worth a latte. What flavor would you like?"

"Caramel?" I couldn't help smiling at the sort-of compliment from Eliska.

"Done." Lina smiled back.

I had played teacher for three more days. On the first day, Eliska had caught me reading an old paperback copy of *The Tempest* that I'd found in the room. I'd sensed her watching me read while the little kids ate their snack and finally looked up. She'd asked me if I had read that book in school, and then we got started talking about the classes I'd taken at Sheldon, and then Eliska had asked if I could read the play with her. She'd pulled up a copy on her iPhone, and we read out loud. The little kids seemed to like to listen as I did different voices for the characters I read. I even made Eliska laugh once. But the new, actual teacher had arrived on Wednesday, just as we were about to load out.

Lina and I sat down with our coffees. "Doesn't Eliska like coffee?" I asked her.

"Not this kind. Too fattening. My sister's very disciplined. I have to be careful, too, but once in a while I cheat." She held up her vanilla latte, which she hadn't ordered nonfat. "Besides, she doesn't want anything to take away from her time with the books. She'll be in here the whole time. I'm going to go shop for clothes, some makeup — she'll still be here. Liska really takes school seriously; she's constantly after my dad to get better teachers for them at the school. But it's not really the way most teachers want to work, traveling around and stuff."

"Is she going to go to college next year? She said she's a senior like me."

"Sore subject." She smiled. "Not so much with me, but with my dad and my brother. If she goes away, we're down to two. Most trapeze teams are at least four. We could get someone else in, but Eddie's kind of . . . challenging to work with. And he and Dad like that it's the Flying Vranas. My mom's family were trapeze people way back. My mom died when I was ten," she added. "Cancer."

"I'm so sorry," I said, swallowing past the lump in my throat and trying not to think about my dad. "That must've been really hard."

"Yeah. Liska took it the hardest, I think." She shook her head and sat up a little straighter, and I could tell she wanted to change the subject. "But she seemed to really like reading that play with you."

As if summoned, Eliska appeared in front of us. "Hi. Lexi? Can I ask you to do something?"

"Sure," I said.

"You were talking the other day about that English class you had last year that was so great. Could you maybe recommend some of the books you read in that class for me to read? I'd just like to . . . I'd like to read some of them."

"Of course," I told her, standing. "Let's go to fiction and I'll show you some good ones. Some famous ones that aren't too dull." I smiled. I looked back at Lina.

"Go ahead," she said with a laugh. "I'll meet you guys back here in about an hour and a half."

I led the way to the fiction section and began pulling books off the shelves for Eliska.

"Okay, so you should probably read something by Jane Austen," I began, pulling down a copy of *Pride and Prejudice*. "You may not like it — not everybody gets Jane — but I love her."

"What are her books about?" Eliska asked, giving the girl-in-a-bonnet cover a dubious look.

"Just read it," I told her. "I can't describe it." I handed her *Wuthering Heights* next, then *Heart of Darkness*, then *Brave New World* and *Hamlet*. "I'm sticking to Brit lit," I told her. "But there are lots of American authors, too. There're too many!" I stepped back from the shelves. "How big is your book budget?"

"I can probably buy about six," Eliska said. "So one more. Can you pick just one?"

"I have some back at the trailer, too," I told her. "You can borrow whatever you want."

"Thanks, Lexi." Eliska smiled that shy smile of hers at me again. Then I settled on *Jane Eyre* and found her a copy.

We sat down to read in the café while we waited for Lina to finish shopping. Eliska dove into *Pride and Prejudice*, and when I heard her laugh out loud, I knew she got it.

As we were pulling back into the parking lot at Europa, Lina turned to me.

"Hey, how attached are you to sleeping in the crew trailer? 'Cause I was thinking, Liska and I each got our own trailer last year, but mine's still a double. I kind of feel bad with you in there with all those guys . . . You want to stay in the spare room in mine instead?"

"YES!" I said, making them both laugh. I raced back to the crew trailer, got my suitcase out of the back, and met Lina outside her trailer. She helped me carry my bag inside and showed me the little room. It was very tiny, with just a twin bed and a small dresser, but compared to the shelf in the crew trailer, it looked like a thousand square feet.

When we were done putting my stuff in the room — in other words, in two minutes — Lina asked if I was ready to head to dinner. I followed her and joined her at her family's usual table. Louie even smiled at me as I came in. Then came another surprise. I had gotten myself a plate of beef stew and sat down when Louie announced to me that he thought I was a good worker. "I can find a new clerk for the novelties wagon like this." He snapped his fingers. "If you're going to stay with us, you should be part of the show."

I was already shaking my head before my brain had time to form words. I had a sudden, very clear mental picture of what I would look like wearing one of Lina's barely-there costumes. As cool as it would be to do something amazing like Lina and Liska, have people applaud for *me*, I knew it just wasn't in the cards.

"I don't really have any talent," I told him. At his raised eyebrow, I added, "I mean, I could never do anything like dancing or performing or whatever. Nothing anyone would want to *watch*."

"I'm not so sure about that. But for a start, what about something on the midway?" he asked.

"Dad thinks you can come up with something creative." Lina smiled. "It's a compliment, really." She waggled her eyebrows, and I laughed.

"I can try to think of something," I told him, and this seemed to satisfy him, because he returned to his beef stew without further comment. I poked at my stew without enthusiasm, wondering what I could possibly do to live up to this idea Louie had about me. He and his children were born into show business. He didn't understand people like me, whose most astounding skill was the ability to be completely invisible.

The show didn't open until the next night, Monday night, so after dinner there was an unexpected lull in my jobs. Lina and her sister went off for yet another rehearsal, probably like the one I'd seen the week before. I walked down the midway, feeling restless. My only other option was a book, but I just wasn't in the mood.

"What's shaking, city girl?" I heard Jamie before I saw

him. He was wrapping an enormous black electrical cord around his arm from elbow to wrist. I walked over to him.

"I have to think of something creative to do in the circus," I told him glumly. "Somehow Louie got this idea about me. I have no idea how."

"I do. You impressed Lina *and* Liska. Not an easy thing to do."

"That's cool, but now I'm sort of stuck. I have no skills whatsoever. But I don't want to let Louie down. And now Lina's even taking me in. And after I just showed up here, like a package sent to the wrong address."

Jamie gave me a sympathetic smile. "Well, you're not a package I'd send back." Before I could get too excited about this comment, he went on to ask, "Lina asked you to move in, huh? What does Liska have to say about it? That's her old room."

"She hasn't said anything."

Jamie looked thoughtful, but answered only with, "Hmm." He walked a few paces away, hung the cord on a hook outside one of the concession trailers, then asked, "So, what are you good at?"

Of all the questions for a completely talent-free person to keep getting. "Nothing that I know of." I tried to smile.

"I'm sure that's not true." Was he flirting with me? Or did he just have so much male charm that the excess just flailed out of him and landed on any girl who happened to be there?

"Well, nothing useful for the circus, anyway," I clarified.

"I mean, I'll do whatever he asks me to. I'm just really hoping not to be on, um, poop detail with Costi again."

Jamie made a face. "Man, that's some rookie treatment, all right." He looked at me for a second. "It's just too bad you're so pale."

"Um. Yes?" I was confused. I mean, I knew I was semi-vampiric in color, but it was the natural result of a life spent almost completely indoors. And I wasn't sure how a tan would help my current talent search.

"No," Jamie said, laughing again. "It wasn't an insult. It's just that Reveka — Madame Tarus — just left us. She's a gypsy fortune teller." He rolled his eyes in a way I guessed was meant to convey his opinions about such things. "If you looked more like a gypsy, maybe you could get that attraction back up and running."

All of a sudden, I had an idea. "Jamie, why *couldn't* I be a pale fortune teller?"

"I was sort of kidding," Jamie said. "But I guess you could be. Do you know what you're doing with . . . that stuff?"

"I'm pretty good at reading tarot cards," I told him, my mind racing. "What else did this Madame Tarus do?" I was thinking about how I'd made up this really cool Divinations Class table for little kids on their Harry Potter day at the local library. But I wasn't about to share this nerdtastic memory with Jamie.

He shrugged. "I only went in there once. I took this girl I met up in Maryland to see Madame T — the girl said she was into that kind of thing . . . But I know she read palms and stuff."

"Maybe I could switch it up a little. And be paler. Also, not a gypsy." I tried not to hold my breath waiting for Jamie to answer. Suddenly, I really wanted this idea to work.

"Yeah, maybe. Hey, stay down here in Florida awhile; maybe you'll not be translucent by the time the winter's over." Jamie laughed.

I didn't point out that I did not, in fact, have anywhere else to go. Even someone as pathetic at flirting as me knew that sounded kind of desperate.

"Maybe I will," I told him. "I could tell Louie about your idea . . ."

"Tell him it's yours. Louie is always impressed with ingenuity. We have a couple more months in the season down here; maybe you could make a go of it by then."

I watched Jamie walk off, wrapping up the cord, and I stood alone on the empty midway.

A couple more months, Jamie had said. A couple more months and the circus would be in winter quarters. The year I had once dreaded for stupid reasons would be over. I didn't need a tarot deck to read my fortune. I wouldn't be going to college.

I wouldn't be going anywhere.

I told Louie the idea the next morning at breakfast. I tried to give Jamie (at least some) of the credit, but Louie didn't seem to hear that part; he said I'd had a great idea. Before lunch, Louie set me up with a small abandoned trailer. It was seriously dirty, but Lina volunteered to help me, saying she was free until her five o'clock call for the first show.

Lina showed up with an impressive array of cleaning supplies. At first I'd waved away the face mask she tried to give me, but I quickly changed my mind as I began to feel woozy and light-headed from the bleach.

We cleaned for hours, our hair tied back in colorful scarves she'd brought. Lina and I laughed as we dug up some of the crazy props, costumes, and unidentifiable items that had found their way into the unused trailer. I found an enormous piece of foam shaped like a hammer and chased Lina with it, calling her a Whac-A-Mole, and then she got the hammer away from me, and I really was the whacked mole, because her aim was way better than mine. We collapsed outside on the grass in front of the trailer, recovering from our hysterics.

Jamie, of course, chose that moment to walk by. I struggled to my feet. Lina got one last big whack in just then, though, so I fell right back down to my knees. That started us both laughing again, and Jamie gave up on whatever he had stopped to say and, shaking his head, kept on walking. A few seconds later, I noticed somebody else watching our show. I recognized the fire-eater from the show rehearsal. As he came closer, I noticed that the skin of his throat was very scarred — occupational hazard, no doubt. He was very slight-statured, with wiry arms poking out of his old-fashioned white sleeveless undershirt, which was neatly tucked into his black pants. He could have walked out of a 1930s circus. I looked away, then peeked again. Nope — he was too tan to be a vampire. I'd read too many YA novels — everybody was a vampire these days.

"Lexi, this is Julian," I heard Lina say, smiling at us both. "Julian, my new friend Lexi. She's going to be joining us for a while."

"Pleased to meet you." I held out my hand, then realized it was still covered in a glove that was pretty nasty from our cleaning job. "Sorry," I said as I peeled off the glove and tried again. Julian bowed very formally over my hand before taking it.

"I am very pleased to meet you, Lex, is it?"

"Lexi," Lina said. "But I hear she changes it sometimes, so I'll have to let you know."

"Ha ha," I said to her. "So, Julian, you're the fire-eater. That's pretty intense. How did you . . . get into fire-eating?" I wasn't sure if it was rude to ask questions about fire-eating, but it was a public spectacle, so I hoped it was fair game. And for some reason, I sort of liked him right off the bat. I remembered my second day at Europa, watching the show with Jamie — Julian had bowed in our direction.

"My father taught me when I was very young. It is a family tradition, so to speak." Julian grinned, as though childhood fire-swallowing was normal, or maybe he was just anticipating my reaction.

I couldn't help it — I gasped involuntarily. "Seriously? How young?"

"Perhaps seven or eight. I was very good at it when I was quite young. It is only when one gets to be closer to your age that . . . distractions get in the way." Julian's hand seemed to go reflexively to his throat as he said this.

"Like girls? Or *a* girl?" Lina asked in a teasing voice.

"Yes, there was a girl. And she was very beautiful. Far too beautiful to have around when one has to keep absolute focus. I once learned a hard lesson when I was about your age."

"Was she worth it — being . . . distracted, I mean?" I asked carefully. It sounded as though this might be a painful story for him — figuratively and literally.

Julian looked surprised. "Oh — no — that's not what I meant at all." Suddenly he smiled a curious smile, and his eyes were far away, unfocused. "No, not at all. If I had to do it once more, I would be distracted all over again. You must always take your chance, Lexi. That is what being young is for. It was a great pleasure to meet you, Lexi. Elina." He bowed briefly to each of us and then walked slowly off.

"Weird," I breathed. "I think that I just got told to not be so boring by a fire-eating circus guy. And your name is Elina?"

"Yep," Lina said. "To both. But call me that again and you're toast." She started chasing me with the foam hammer again, and I didn't get far.

I felt bad later, for laughing, and forgetting, for three whole hours, that my dad died alone in the middle of the street, and that the police couldn't even find me for five hours because I wasn't where I was supposed to be . . .

When it hit me, I was sitting alone in my new closet-size room in Lina's trailer. I'd been lying there trying to sleep for what felt like hours, and the already-close tin walls started to move closer, and I think I started hyperventilating. So I got up off the little bed — I honestly think it might've been a child's mattress; luckily I wasn't overly tall — and slammed out of the trailer as fast as I could.

I was just walking, and there was Jamie, unloading boxes from a truck that had just arrived with some kind of delivery. I hadn't wanted to see anyone, but for some reason when I saw Jamie, and he looked at me, I stopped walking and felt myself willing him to come over to me. For once I didn't want to be invisible. I didn't want to be alone. He took one look at my face and dropped the box he was holding, took my hand, and led me away from the truck.

Jamie led me behind the tiger trailer and dropped my hand, the one he'd grabbed to take me back there. I stood, numb, not knowing what to do with my arms, feeling like they weren't even my arms just then. I started to wrap them protectively around my middle, for lack of anything else to do, but Jamie stopped me, taking a step toward me, standing so close I couldn't pull my arms up without hitting him. He reached up slowly, tucked a stray lock of hair behind my ear. That's how it started.

My heart was beating very fast, and a voice in my head was yelling at me to get out of there, reminding me how no good could come of my racing heart or cute boys who didn't belong to me.

But I forgot to act like a spaz, forgot to overthink everything that was happening, forgot that I pretty much had no idea what I was doing — unlike Jamie, who totally knew what he was doing. I just wanted not to think about New York.

So I closed my eyes and let go. It was like dancing, just letting him lead. And he was kissing me, and I was kissing him back. And then it was over, and all the awkwardness came rushing back, and I stepped back away from Jamie. I started walking, then running, back to my little room in Lina's trailer.

Somehow, Lina knew, right away, about me and Jamie.

"So, you and Jamie, huh?" Lina asked, handing me a box of Honey Nut Cheerios.

I felt my face get red and hot. "Um. Yeah. It was kind of an accident." I poured some cereal into my bowl and handed the box back.

"I probably should have warned you; he's a bit of a player." She looked at me before turning around to put the box away. "I guess I thought you'd figure that out."

"He definitely seems like one," I said, nodding. "Like I said, kind of accidental. I don't have any, like, delusions about him."

"Smart girl." She laughed as she turned back around and added milk to her bowl, but there was something weird about the sound. Was this about Jamie? Did the same stupid musical-chairs dating go on here just like back at Sheldon?

"Yeah, I'm kind of challenged when it comes to all that stuff," I said. "Under normal circumstances I'm like a nun or something. But I kind of had a meltdown last night." I was looking at Lina, trying to figure out if she was mad or if something really was up. But she was keeping her eyes on her Cheerios. Because those are so interesting to look at.

"I guess you took Julian's advice," Lina said next, skipping over what I'd said about my meltdown. "You took your chance."

She looked at me then, and winked and smiled, then flopped down on her little love seat in the middle of the trailer and flipped on her tiny TV. She started chattering about her performance with Eliska and Eddie the night before. She seemed to be acting like normal Lina, but I knew it was just that: acting. I had done a lot of that kind of acting myself in the last year.

Perfect. I found someone who could be a real friend, who even let me move in with her, and that's when I completely jump off my normal track for five seconds and manage to make out with the cutest boy in maybe all of Florida . . . and he's the guy she likes.

Well, I wasn't ever going to go near Jamie again — not like that. I wasn't that girl. I swallowed hard, remembering that night back in New York when I *had* been that girl. And anyway, it wasn't likely that Jamie would even be interested in kissing me again, not with so many new distractions buying tickets every night in every new town.

This was really the perfect start to my new job as fortune teller, giving other people advice. About things like love.

CHAPTER TEN

STICKY RICE/STICKY CONVERSATION

"It's just another day, nothing in my way
I don't wanna go, I don't wanna stay"
— KEANE, "NOTHING IN MY WAY"

112 Bowery — Thursday, September 23

One more year. One more year. This had become my mantra over the course of this long, sweltering summer. My dad had been gone almost all the time. Bailey and Eli had been in the Hamptons. And now that they were back, they were different. They kept acting weird — at least around me.

I wished so badly that I was going to college this year instead of next year. I wanted to start over, be somebody else. I was so tired of being invisible Xandra. None of the forty-seven people in my class noticed or cared what I did. To be fair, it was kind of mutual — I didn't adore most of them, either. I was so ready to reinvent myself. Talk more in class. Stop skulking around to cult films and used bookstores and complaining about stupid people. I wanted to just have, I don't know, fun — for a change.

I felt like in college there would be some kind of a map

of how to do that. Places I'd have to be at specific times, new faces to meet and memorize. But until then, how was I supposed to shake things up? Did I just strike up conversations with strangers? This was New York: That could end badly.

So I kept skulking around the city, mostly by myself, eating food on sticks or in little foil envelopes — because food by yourself in a restaurant is just sad. It's okay with a book, but eating and reading is not that easy. And I'd been to every used bookstore in a forty-block radius, and anyway, I was sick of books about interesting people — people who had actual lives. Instead, I watched real people go about their real lives, taking advantage of my invisibility, noticing people's quirks, the way they talked, everything.

I think my dad finally noticed my extreme funk, because he made a big deal about us having dinner together that night. He seemed pretty intent on my being psyched about the plan, so I'd promised him about six times that I'd be home at seven, ready for father-daughter eating and bonding.

I got home from school early and headed for my room. I usually liked hanging out in there. I had concert posters covering most of the available surfaces, and the bedspread I'd wanted for a year: black with little silver embroidered stars. I still had my eye on the matching curtains, but for now I was making do with some purple silky ones I found in a little store on Seventh Street. I had two sets of twinkle lights, in the shape of little purple gargoyles, strung together and draped over the window ledge and the little Chinese screen in the corner. Technically, they were supposed to be a Halloween decoration, but I liked them all the time. The rest of the room, minus the bed, was almost completely taken up by bookshelves.

But somehow I didn't feel like being in my room today. It seemed more like the world's smallest and worst organized library and less like the haven I needed. So I sat out on the fire escape until it started to drizzle.

I was setting out plates and cups in the kitchen when Gavin came in a few minutes later, shaking his damp hair, a destroyed denim jacket over his perpetual T-shirt (this one was for the band Minus the Bear). I was sure he got it for free; my dad hasn't bought clothes since around 1994. Unfortunately, he was wearing jeans with the denim jacket.

"Dad, you do realize you're wearing a denim tuxedo?"

"Aw, Lex, give me a break. This is probably the closest I will ever come to a tuxedo, so maybe you should just enjoy my sartorial splendor and be thankful that I brought Thai."

"Ooh, Thai. Okay, wear what you want. Is it from Sticky Rice?"

"Who do you think you're dealing with? Thanks for setting the table."

"I was just getting out the plates. Did someone die? Since when do we eat at the table?" I paused for a moment in horror as an idea occurred to me. "You didn't invite some new girlfriend, did you?" Every once in a while, Gavin got serious enough with some woman that she insisted on meeting his daughter. I got the feeling it was pretty much never his idea. The last one, Cherie, had been a year or so ago. That had been a fun evening. She spent all night telling me why meat was murder as we all sat around the table not eating the meatloaf I had tried so hard to make edible.

"No." Dad frowned at me. "I meant what I said before. We haven't been spending enough time together. I wanted us to just have dinner. No ulterior motive."

He actually looked kind of hurt, so now I felt like a terrible daughter. I didn't know what to say then, so I went to the fridge and got out the iced-tea pitcher while Gavin got out the cartons of food.

"So what's been going on with you lately? Anything new?" he asked.

"The complete and utter absence of anything new. What about you?"

"God, Lex — sorry, Xandra. Sometimes I can't believe you are growing up in this city and you can't think of anything good to do. If I'd lived here when I was seventeen, man, what I would've gotten into."

I shot him a look. "So you want me to act how I think you would have if you'd lived in New York when you were seventeen?" I raised an eyebrow at him and waited for the mental pictures to sink in.

"*No!* I mean, you're a *girl* . . ."

"Great logic, Gavin. But you can't have it both ways. I hang out in my room and read books. You should be the happiest dad in America. Or at least in the five boroughs."

"I don't care about me being happy, Lex — I care about *you* being happy. And it worries me that you're . . . not."

Wow. I struggled to swallow the dumpling I had tried to inhale at exactly the wrong moment. It was one thing to be sort of bummed and depressed; it was another thing for your father to sit you down over Thai takeout from your favorite restaurant and announce that he could tell you were unhappy.

"I'm not super-extra happy right now," I told him, once I got past the dumpling and the shock. "But I will be, when I get to college, which is really soon. High school is just . . . high school."

"So you always tell me. I kind of liked high school. No responsibilities, no job, time with your friends." He stopped to look at me. "But maybe that's the problem. Eli and Bailey have kind of cut you out of the picture a little bit, huh?"

"A lot bit. But it's okay!" I rushed to add. "I mean, they're dating. He really likes her. And he deserves it."

Dad acted like he hadn't heard me. "I never expected Eli to be like this. I thought more of him than that." He shook his head sadly, for the moment looking more like a regular dad than he usually did. I could picture him addressing Eli, telling him, "I'm so disappointed in you." Then I pictured myself saying that to Eli. Because, I realized in that moment, I *was* kind of disappointed in him.

"I know he really fell for Bailey," Gavin began carefully, looking into his nearly empty noodle carton as if there were something really interesting down there in the bottom. "But he was your friend first. You two have been friends for a long time."

"You make it sound as though I've been cast aside." I gestured expansively with my arm, narrowly missing knocking the remains of the green chicken curry off the table.

"That's how you've been acting these last few months," Dad said quietly. "It's not like this is a situation that's going on in my head."

Ugh. He had a point there. "So what do you suggest I do?"

"What do you want to do?"

"Part of me wants to confront Eli. Tell him how I feel, everything out in the open, all that. Part of me wants to just make it through the rest of this year." I pretty much already knew which part was going to win. By the look on Gavin's face, he knew, too.

"I just never thought Eli would be such a jerk," he muttered.

"Dad! I thought you liked Eli."

"Used to," Dad said around a mouthful of sticky rice. "Until he made my little girl sad."

I felt the sudden prick of tears behind my eyes at my father's unusual mushiness.

Gavin wiped his mouth with a napkin as he stood up. "You'll take care of all this?" He gestured at the mass of cartons and the noodles we'd dribbled onto the table. "I have to go back to the station."

And as fast as that, the moment of mush was over.

CHAPTER ELEVEN

THINGS WERE GOING PRETTY WELL FOR ABOUT A MINUTE, SO IT WAS TIME FOR A MEAN BUT GORGEOUS GUY TO START YELLING AT ME FOR NO REASON

"All left hands and accidents, the size of your life
I didn't see you coming out the corner of my eye"
— THE PROMISE RING, "SIZE OF YOUR LIFE"

Winter Springs, Florida — Monday, October 25

I was sitting on the grass outside the trailer, trying to sew two smaller pieces of fabric together to make a curtain. It smelled like rain, but it was still very warm. Even the ground was warm. All of a sudden, the sky darkened, and I stabbed myself with the needle.

I realized as I sucked the blood from my finger that there

was someone standing over me. He was blocking the light, so his features were indistinct, but I could tell right away that he was handsome. I mean, ridiculous. Square jaw, shiny black hair. Muscles bulging, visible though he wore a white button-up shirt.

"Who the hell are you?" he bellowed at me without preamble.

I always want to react appropriately to rude people. Later, I can always think of the perfect response. But my tragic flaw is that I always, always pause for just a second before I do or say anything. And with that second the moment passes. I spent that crucial second gaping at him instead of speaking, and he moved around me so that I could see his face clearly, by this time half hoping he had a beaky nose or bad skin. No such luck.

"I said, who the hell are you? Are you deaf?" he snarled at me.

"I'd rather be deaf than be like . . . you are." Wow. That was the lamest comeback in the history of forever.

"I was told my mother's replacement was here. But Louie must have gone insane," he mused aloud, as if I weren't even sitting there. "He's run off a seasoned professional, someone he'd made a commitment to, and hired a rude child."

I got to my feet, struggling a bit with the fabric that wanted to tangle itself around my ankles. "Child?" I snapped. "Look here, buddy. I don't know who the hell you think *you* are, but let me tell you something: I am not rude, and I am not a child. You are the one who's rude, you big, rude . . ." I sputtered, unable to think of a word horrible enough that I had the guts to utter just then.

"Big, rude what? Nothing to say? Times must be tough if they think people will pay money to get advice from an unpleasant teenager."

He *looked* young, but he talked like he was forty-five. "Unpleasant! Have you *met* yourself? What have I ever done to you?"

"What have you done? Oh, nothing. Just what your kind always does. You show up — where you're not wanted, by the way — and take the job of someone born to this life, someone with nowhere else to go. I've known your kind before, again and again: a bored young dilettante who just wants to stick it to mommy and daddy, so you run off to join the circus. You'll stay maybe one season, if Louie's lucky. And then you'll go back to your real life. Tell me, what did Daddy do that was so terrible that you just had to run away? Ground you for the weekend? Did he take away your credit card?"

I knew I shouldn't, even in the moment I knew it. But he'd pushed me pretty far.

"He died!" I heard myself scream, and I watched all the color drain from his handsome face.

And then I burst into tears.

When I got a tentative hold on myself, I looked at the guy again — who still seemed stricken — and then I started crying all over again, feeling like a really bad person for saying what I'd said about my dad, all to sort of win an argument, really. And then I just cried harder.

It took a couple of seconds for me to realize *where* I was crying — in his arms, the arms of the guy who had just been yelling at me. After I pulled myself together for a second time, I blew my nose on one of the spare pieces of material that he handed me, and I looked at him. I took a step back, and he lowered his arms. All of his anger definitely seemed to be gone, but he still stood tensely; probably he was afraid to say or do anything for fear I would start sobbing again.

He ran a hand through his thick hair, looked away and exhaled, then met my eyes. "I am so sorry. So sorry! Please forgive me. I was just worried . . . My mother was turned out from here, it seems. And I didn't know. I don't actually know where she is, so I was upset, you understand . . . But that's no excuse for what I said to you. Please accept my apology."

I met his eyes. He was one of those people who had a stare that was just a little too intense. And the freaking movie-star looks weren't helping, either. I was so caught up with the staring, I hadn't noticed he'd extended his hand. I took it, and his hand closed around mine, very warm. He placed his other hand across my forearm.

"I'm Nicolae," he told me. "The jerk." He smiled a little, ruefully. "You are Lexi?" He said his name like *nick-o-lye*, but there was an exotic, foreign lilt to the way he pronounced it, though I didn't hear it in the rest of his words.

"Yes." I remembered to breathe. "I guess you heard all about me," I added a little dryly, wiping my eyes of the last remnants of tears.

"Not all," he amended softly. "Again, please forgive me. It's just, growing up in this life, I've dealt with so many spoiled brats who come here to run away from something."

"Well, in point of fact, I guess that includes me, too. But I didn't actually have anywhere else to go . . ." I trailed off, not sure why I was starting to be in such a confiding mood all of a sudden with the guy who'd just been insulting me. I used picking up the fabric pieces as an excuse to get my bearings. He bent to help me, and our hands brushed again, and I noticed that he seemed electrically charged. But maybe I was just imagining things in my weirdly overemotional state.

"Obviously your situation is . . . quite different from what I assumed. I should not have assumed. I was angry, and you got in the way."

I stopped myself from pointing out that I had actually been sitting in a quiet corner of a field, sewing, out of the way of everybody in pretty much the entire universe.

"Do you need some help with these?" He gestured with his armful of fabric.

"I'll take them," I told him, leaning forward to catch the pile. "Thanks," I mumbled. I felt a bit weird thanking him after the tirade of a few moments before.

I turned away to take the armload into the trailer

and was surprised when he followed. He looked around inside.

"You will need some things," he observed. "To make this work. I'll bring them tomorrow."

With that, he was gone. I stood in the middle of the trailer and held the armful of fabric in midair for a few seconds, trying to figure out what had just happened. I realized as I stood there that if this guy had a problem with circus newcomers, he would *not* have approved of my mother.

And what had dear old Mom been running away from? Oh yeah — me.

CHAPTER TWELVE

DEFINE INTERESTING

*"In the end I was the mean girl
Or somebody's in-between girl"*
— NEKO CASE, "HOLD ON, HOLD ON"

13 Broome Street — Tuesday, September 28

Lots of times, I will imagine that there's a fire and I have to figure out what to take with me. If the fire were right now, at Sheldon Prep, that would be an easy answer — the entire contents of my backpack and a song in my heart (assuming the fire is like a total conflagration and not just enough to make everything moist and smell like smoke). I pictured Dad's sad face and my faux-sympathy for his private school plans, now gone up in literal smoke.

I sniffed the air surreptitiously from my usual seat in the extreme back of my AP Gov classroom. Not even a hint of smoke. I was situated very deliberately behind Georgie Latimer, who was a linebacker, or some kind of backer, in football — one of those big dudes, anyway. Nestled safely behind Georgie, I had managed the first three weeks of school without Mr. Ness even noticing me. I figured I was probably good for the rest of the semester.

So I went back to planning what I would take if there were a fire at our apartment. First, obviously, my laptop — with all my music. Second, both iPods, and my Bose headphones, if for some reason they weren't actually in my ears at the time. One of the best inventions of the modern age has to be really amazing headphones. If it hadn't been for headphones, for example, I would probably be hearing Mr. Ness lecturing about something truly horrible, like supply-side economics, instead of what I was actually hearing: a really nice early nineties independent scene playlist, with a little Built to Spill, some Pavement, a dash of Promise Ring.

Argh! Suddenly Georgie Latimer was out of his seat and on the move — that was a first. I hurried to yank the headphones off of my ears, fiddling with my notebook for a diversion. In my failed attempt to be cool, I knocked my notebook off my desk. Mr. Ness gave me a brief look before continuing his lecture. Unfortunately, now he knew I was back here. I could only hope he would forget. At least it was only a one-semester course.

I started putting my notebook back together — it was the only one I used, and I mostly used it for nonschool stuff, like playlists and shopping lists. But there was an envelope in it that I hadn't seen before. In fact, I don't think I'd ever seen any envelopes of any kind in with my notebooks. Gavin was not really the type to buy office supplies, and we paid almost all our bills online. I mean, we got mail, of course, but I tossed most of it before even going upstairs. This wasn't a reused envelope; it was a new white one with only one letter written on it: X. It didn't take me too many seconds to figure out, even though one letter isn't much of a handwriting sample. It was from Eli.

I looked around like a spy or something, even though neither Eli nor Bailey had this class with me. And in the next second I called myself an idiot, because why should it matter who might see me open an envelope that I found in my own notebook, with my own name on it? I ripped it open and pulled out the single sheet of notebook paper inside. It was folded three ways, like it was some sort of official legal document — *so* Eli. But he had only written three sentences on it, in pencil. It said:

> X,
>
> *I have something I want to talk to you about. I have sort of an interesting question for you. Meet me today after school on your fire escape?*
> *Eli*

Today? How long had this thing been in here? Not long, probably — I dropped it at least once a day, although usually I was more careful in my government class hidey-hole. Luckily Eli had picked a meeting place where I could go and hang without feeling stupid. Although why had he slipped me this note, rather than just asking me?

I went straight home after school. Nothing unusual there. It's not like I didn't do anything after school ever — I mean, no one's getting out of having at least a couple of extracurriculars for their college applications, right? But I didn't have anything going on right then — yearbook hadn't started meeting yet, and neither had literary magazine. So it was back to the Bowery for me every day at three o'clock. I almost always walked the fourteen blocks home, unless there was a downpour or something.

The walk was uneventful and gave me a chance to listen to the rest of the playlist I had started in AP Gov. I realized it needed more up-tempo songs. It was pretty much a suicide mix. This realization reminded me of the uncomfortable dinner with Gavin last week. I had to snap out of this funk, or Gavin was gonna institute weekly dinners/serious conversations with me.

When I got home, I threw my bag on the kitchen table and stomped down the hall to my room. I put my Nano on its speakers and hit play, then sat down on my bed and was pulling off my tights when I heard Eli yelp, "Xandra!"

"What the — Eli! You scared me!"

Eli had cheated — he had crawled inside my room instead of staying on the fire escape, and he was sitting on my window seat. Hence his unprecedented view of my, er, tights-removal situation, and my almost-coronary.

"God, Eli! How did you get home so much faster than me? Did you, like, run?"

Eli shook his head, though he had been kind of shaking his head in a dazed way since I'd noticed him. But the shaking got a bit more vigorous, and in another couple of seconds he regained his verbal faculties. "Yes — I mean, no — I didn't run or walk. Bailey's mom picked her up and they gave me a ride on their way."

"My apartment was on their way? Sounds kind of unlikely."

"What do you even mean? Bailey's mom and dad are just regular people, like our parents — like our families."

I gave him a look, kicking the rest of my tights off. "Eli, on your way out, take a look at my apartment. Then, when you go home, look at yours. Step three, when you go home with Bailey tomorrow or whatever, open your eyes. Then maybe get back to me on that whole *regular* theory."

"You're so critical of Bailey's family because they have money. What's up with that?"

"Eli, I'm critical of pretty much everything. You used to be, too, not that long ago."

He just looked at me for a second without talking, Neko Case filling up the silence. "You mean before Bailey," he said finally.

"Shoot, this song's way too new." I got up and walked over to my tiny desk, picking up my laptop, meaning to fix the playlist and hopefully change the subject.

"God, X. You are so concerned with classifying everything, making sure every song is in its perfect little playlist slot. But when it comes to actually *talking* . . ."

I whirled around. "So talk, Eli. Seriously, speak. I mean, you must actually have something to say to me for a change. I'm not really sure why you had to hide a note in my stuff today and make, like, an *appointment* to talk to me, but whatever. Go ahead — what's this interesting thing you have to tell me?"

"Ask you," he said, very quietly. "It was something I wanted to ask you. And I didn't hide that note today. I put it in there yesterday. You didn't come home until after I had to be home myself. I waited."

I sat down then, across from where he sat on the window seat, in my little desk chair. "Oh — I'm sorry. I wondered how long the note had been in there. But, Eli, we just . . . We used to talk *all the time*, is the thing . . ." I stopped, feeling stupid tears pricking my eyes, feeling stupid period.

"I know, X. And that's kind of what I wanted to ask you. I mean, I know things have been different, that we don't see each other as much. This summer —"

"You were gone."

"I was with Bailey, yeah. I remember. That's not what I wanted. I mean . . ." Eli stopped, standing up and starting to pace. This was my best friend for almost my whole life, in my room, *pacing*, like he was working up the nerve to talk to me.

"Eli, whatever it is, say it. I'm a big girl. I can take it."

Eli stopped his pacing and stood in front of me, looking at me but not speaking. Just as it was about to get mega-weird, and I was just going to have to say something to make it stop, he opened his mouth to speak.

"It's nothing — forget it. I thought you might be mad at

me about this summer. About going away. I felt like I owed you an apology or something."

"Oh-kay," I began slowly. "No, you don't owe me anything — I'm not upset or mad or anything like that." *Liar!*

"Oh, well, good. I just wanted to make sure. Cool. Well, I'll see you at school."

With that, he was gone, halfway down the fire escape before I could make fun of his whole "cool" situation. Not only had he taken to pacing in front of me, he was talking to me like I was a total stranger. Better and better.

It wasn't until about a half an hour later, as I stared without comprehension at the pages of my math textbook, that I remembered the note. I picked it up and read it again, just to be sure. Yep, there it was: *I have sort of an interesting question for you.* Whatever that question had been, Eli hadn't asked it.

CHAPTER THIRTEEN

BECAUSE I'M STUPID

"How come I end up where I started?
How come I end up where I went wrong?"
— RADIOHEAD, "15 STEP"

Orlando, Florida — Saturday, October 30

"He comes and goes," Lina said, answering the question I had tried not to let on I was asking. "His mom used to be here, so he would come check on her. And of course he used to work here, too."

I tried to sound nonchalant, moving my right foot and presenting Lina with my left; she was painting my toenails a dark metallic blue.

"What did he do here?"

"Um, everything. His family's all performers way back. Mostly acrobats and wire work and stuff. His mother used to fly when she was young. I know he did a bunch of acts when he was a kid. But he also ran a midway show for a while. Like a strongman, with the big hammer? We don't have it anymore. It takes somebody really strong to make any money at it. And somebody who really knows how to reel in the townies."

I smiled. "So how long has he been gone? From Europa, I mean."

"Girl of a thousand questions today, aren't we?" Lina wagged her eyebrows at me. "This sudden curiosity about Nick wouldn't have anything to do with him being freakishly hot, would it?"

I blushed. "I told you, he was super rude to me. I was just curious, that's all. No big deal."

"Nope, clearly you don't care at all." Lina rolled her eyes. I was paying close attention, but even though she'd called him freakishly hot, there was no weirdness in her like there'd been with Jamie. Jamie, who I was definitely putting behind me, no matter how many shirtless smiles he gave me.

And Lina was right about me, of course. I did seem to be almost obsessed already, and I'd only spoken to Nick twice. I was definitely the stupidest person in the world. Nick Tarus was clearly older than me, a hundred times prettier than me, and on top of that, any niceness he displayed toward me was definitely the result of my making him feel like a monster.

"I should probably warn you about Nick," Lina went on. She seemed very serious for a moment, then I heard her tinkling laugh. "But then, you knew about Jamie, and that didn't stop you."

I grabbed the pillow from under my knee and threw it at her.

"Don't worry about it," she managed between laughs. "Jamie has that effect on everybody. I don't think there's ever been anybody who resisted him for long." Lina seemed normal about Jamie now — maybe I had imagined the weirdness before?

"You?" I dared to ask.

"Present company excluded," she confirmed, with exaggerated smugness.

I shook my head. "Well, I am done with boys. I've said it before, but I really, really mean it this time."

"Good thing Nick is more like a *man*, then." Lina threw the pillow back at my head.

"You suck!" I hopped up to avoid her and destroyed three toes' worth of metallic blue.

I tried to sound casual as I asked the next question, like the answer didn't matter to me. "So how old is he, anyway?"

"He's my age," she answered. "I mean, I think he's a couple months older than me, but he's probably still nineteen. He inherited some money from his dad when he died a few years back, and then Nick went to Miami. I know he bought some real estate and stuff. He's got this club — his cousin's name is on it and everything, since Nick's underage. But it's Nick who owns the building." Lina handed me the nail polish remover and threw a bag of cotton balls at my head. "Actually, I said I should warn you about Nick, but he's really a good guy. I mean, he's solid, you know. Always taking care of his mom, and his cousins — everybody, really. He's beautiful, so I'm guessing he's got, or you know, had a lot of girls, but . . ."

"Yeah, I'll bet," I told her, trying to make her stop theorizing about Nick and girls.

Liska saved me by walking in then and asking Lina if she was ready for practice. She smiled vaguely at me, but looked irritated that Lina wasn't ready.

I looked from one sister to the other as they hashed out what time they'd agreed on for practice. It was hard to believe that they were sisters. I knew they were very close — I'd seen as much during the weeks I had been here. They had to be, to work together so high off the ground. These sisters *had* to trust each other. But their personalities were so different. Liska was so quiet and seemed almost cold, where Lina was warm and cheerful.

I was left alone with Liska while Lina went to change. Liska sat down and picked up one of the magazines Lina left strewn all over. Liska seemed a little frostier than usual toward me. I realized suddenly that I'd been taking Lina away from her pretty often in the last week or so. I felt bad that I'd been sucking up Lina's time and attention gratefully, not thinking about anything or anybody else.

Lina appeared back in the room and announced she was ready.

"So will you?" I heard Liska saying, and she was looking expectantly at me. I realized she'd been talking to me.

"Sure — of course." I had no idea what I'd just promised her, but I followed her, and Lina grabbed my arm and fell into step beside me.

I tried to murmur very quietly without moving my lips or alerting Liska to the fact that I hadn't really been listening to her, "WhatdidIjustsayyesto?"

"Wha-huh-what, mushmouth?" Lina responded in her loudest voice.

"Never mind." I gave up and figured I'd just see when I got there.

When we got to the ring in its present location — I was getting surprisingly used to picking up and moving every week — their brother, Eddie, was there waiting for them, looking annoyed. He didn't acknowledge my existence, and neither Lina nor her sister introduced me, so I just followed his lead. I watched Liska shed her cardigan sweater, put some chalk or something on her hands, and climb up the long ladder. When she was halfway up and mostly out of earshot, I asked Lina if I was supposed to do something.

Lina gave me a funny look. "What would you do? Liska just wants an opinion on our new trick. She's kind of a perfectionist."

"Why does she want my opinion?" I was incredulous.

Lina turned her head thoughtfully to the side for a moment, while she put the same stuff her sister had used on her hands. "I think she's been watching you set up your fortune-telling act, and she's impressed with you. She's seen how you've been paying attention to every tiny little detail — like how you made me take you to fourteen stores looking for fabric and stuff? That's the kind of opinion she wants."

Lina started climbing up the rope ladder, but I stopped her. "Wait! What music plays while you guys do this? I can't remember what it was."

"Just 'The Three-Ring Fanfare.' It repeats for most of the ring stuff."

"It *repeats*?" That seemed kind of lame.

"Just how it's done, I guess." She started back up.

"Can I hear it while I see it?"

"Ralph!" Lina yelled, very suddenly and very loudly. A tiny old man I'd never laid eyes on before emerged from the shadows of the ring. "Play the fanfare, will ya?"

"Course, Miss Lina," came his soft voice in reply. I looked around surreptitiously then, wondering how many other people lurked unseen in the shadows, awaiting a random shouted command. Freaky.

I heard the traditional-sounding circus music begin to play, and Lina finally joined her sister in midair. They both started out on the same side, on a little crow's nest sort of stand — Lina never talked about the act, so I didn't know the proper terminology, just the little bit Jamie had mentioned that day I'd watched the whole show.

I watched Lina and Liska build up speed, and their surly brother caught them every time, making it look effortless. They really did look like they were flying. It was hard to tell the two sisters apart up there; if it hadn't been for Liska's lighter hair, I couldn't have done it.

I watched them cross and soar, and it was breathtaking. The music, however, was not. It was too jarring, too discordant and crash-y to match what the siblings did up there. I just hoped Liska really wanted my advice. Because I actually had some for her.

I had spent every night over the past week making the playlist for outside the Fortune Trailer. (Since the attraction didn't have an official name, that's what I'd been calling it. Then Jamie had shown up with a painted sign — I guess one of the crew guys was really good at painting lettering — and so now the name was official.) Luckily, most of the space on my laptop hard drive was filled with music, so I had a lot to choose from. I had worked hard to choose the perfect music to get people to come up and see the trailer and to want to have their tarot cards read. I thought the challenge was to strike the right balance between familiar and new or unusual music that created the proper atmosphere.

"So, what do you think?" Liska asked me once she was on the ground. Lina was fiddling with the net behind her, but Eddie had vanished — as usual.

"I love the double-switch thing you added in the middle."

Liska looked gratified that I'd noticed. I had paid very close attention. If there had been a nonobvious way to take notes, I would have done it.

"But," I continued, "and this is just an idea, I think you need different music. What you're using now doesn't do justice to your act. You need something . . . well, something newer, for a start. You guys are young, you're smoking hot. What you're doing is way more awesome than twenty revolutions on the Hurricane. But everybody lines up to do that because the music pulls them in."

"You think we should use Jamie's music?" Liska asked, sounding more than a little incredulous. Or maybe horrified.

"Well, first of all, that's not just Jamie's music. It's mostly whatever is top-twenty on iTunes right now. And, no, I think that's too obvious. But somewhere between Hurricane music and that decrepit old circus dirge . . ."

Liska stood perfectly still for a moment. Lina had come up behind her sister and seemed to be holding her breath. I held my breath, too, hoping I hadn't offended either of them. Finally, Liska smiled. Like, an actual smile. Not a grin, maybe, but it was a start.

"You may be right." She nodded.

And then she shocked me completely.

"Will you find us something new?"

It took me a couple of seconds to recover, but I quickly said yes.

Liska continued to thaw at a pretty rapid rate after that, and soon it was the three of us instead of just me and Lina. She even started helping me with the Fortune Trailer. I was nervous about actually taking people's money for something I used to do for my friends for entertainment. But I didn't want to let Louie down. If this experiment failed, I was determined that it would be the best-looking failed attraction on the grounds.

I was mostly nervous about what to wear. I'd tried on a

hundred things, but nothing felt right. I felt like an idiot imposter in everything. Lina found a bunch of stuff she liked at Goodwill, but the clothes smelled musty, so then I felt like a musty idiot imposter. But Lina had promised to take me back to the mall the next day, and she'd promised me a makeover that would make me at least *look* fortune-tellery.

Nick had been as good as his word and brought me some of his mom's stuff a couple of days ago. I replaced the rickety card table I had been set to use with the small round table made of dark, glossy wood that Nick brought. It had very ornately carved legs. He also brought me a pretty real-looking crystal ball. I must've looked a little panicked at that one, because he was quick to assure me that it was just window dressing (in other words, no hundred-year curse on my head if I broke it). He also brought me some old, occult-looking books, a few delicate, intricately beaded scarves to decorate with, and some wooden candleholders. And finally, he presented me with a ring.

"This was my grandmother's," he told me.

"Your mother wouldn't want you to —"

"It was my *paternal* grandmother's," he added with a wicked grin. "My mother hated her. She would stomp this under her heel before she wore it. Anyway, my grandmother was Romanian. Well, in point of fact, she was Romany — a gypsy. And a fortune teller."

"Is your mom —"

"Yes to the second — no to the first. My mother is Czech, like the Vranas — Louie and Lina and Eliska — and

Eddie. If it makes you feel any better that you're not following in the footsteps of an actual *gypsy* fortune teller," he teased. He'd straddled the tiny little art deco chair he'd brought, and he seemed to take up all the room in the trailer.

I fidgeted with the candleholders.

"I'm really glad you found your mom," I told him. Lina had filled me in on the story. Nick's mom had been staying with an old friend in Miami. She'd had a blowup with Louie — apparently they both had pretty bad tempers, and Nick's mom had gotten sick of him and of the circus. She had left her son a message that she had been fired, then gone off the grid. It kind of sounded like she'd used Nick to get some revenge on Louie, probably knowing he'd show up and go ballistic, which I had gotten to witness firsthand.

"Yeah, me too. She's my mother, and I love her. But she drives me crazy." He shook his head. "Come here," he told me, holding up the ring. I stood over him as he straddled the chair, and he reached up and took my hand. When he touched me I felt that same charge I'd felt the first time. He slipped the ring on my finger and then raised my hand and kissed the back of it.

I expected him to laugh after that, since he was obviously kidding with me. But he just kept looking into my eyes. I broke eye contact first, confused, and looked down at the ring on my finger. It was a huge, milky-crystal orb overlaid with intricate brass filigree. He reached up and twirled a lock of my hair around his fingers, then let it go. I forgot to breathe.

"You could be a gypsy with that dark hair. But not with those eyes of yours." His voice was low, and I took a step closer to him. I wasn't even sure how it happened.

My iPod was playing on my little speakers as always. I can't exist without music. A slow song by Damien Jurado was playing, and as Nick stood up, for a moment we stood very close, and didn't speak. Neither of us moved for a long moment. This time he broke away first, telling me he had to go, he'd see me soon, and then he was gone.

Like I said: stupid.

CHAPTER FOURTEEN

ON THE LIST OF THINGS I *SO* DO NOT WANT TO HEAR ABOUT IN DETAIL — THIS IS NUMBER ONE

"Is there a line that I could write,
sad enough to make you cry?
All the lines you wrote to me were lies"
— GIN BLOSSOMS, "FOUND OUT ABOUT YOU"

Somewhere Below 14th Street — Wednesday, September 29

I have an actual list of worst days ever. There was one right after my mom left — one in particular, because there were a lot of bad days back then. But this one day, Gavin listened to the song "Found Out About You" by the Gin Blossoms on repeat. Part of the tragedy is Gavin Ryan listening to the Gin Blossoms. I mean, it's a pretty good song (until you hear it on repeat for twenty-four hours). But it's really not his scene at all, is one thing. For another, he listened to it on repeat for *twenty-four hours*. The song itself was sort of perfect for his situation. But when it's your mom, who you love (or who you used to love) who's the lying, betraying [fill in whatever you want here — I hate her now] . . . Anyway, it wasn't so awesome at the time. To this day, if I even hear a song that I think might be the Gin Blossoms, I run.

Today is now on this list of days, and it's moving up with a bullet. For a start, I went shopping. With Barbie — I mean, Bailey. I didn't plan to — it just sort of happened. I got sucked into the gravitational pull that is Bailey.

We got out early on every other Wednesday for the teachers to have meetings or whatever, and Bailey grabbed me after fifth period, and somehow I was roped into shopping. It's not that I don't like to shop. I appreciate the consumer marketplace. I mostly like books and CDs, old jewelry, and when planning to ask for a birthday/Christmas/I-will-clean-the-apartment-for-a-month present, something shiny at the Apple Store.

Bailey, though, she likes clothes and shoes, in a seemingly infinite and endless variety and supply. It's not that I wear sackcloth, but I guess I tend to go for something made of denim on the bottom and a T-shirt on top unless I have to look a little nicer, and then it's a plain black shirt. And I have one really simple black dress that looks pretty good on me, and it has worked for every single dress-up situation in my life so far. Bailey is a different story — a different genre. So we had already been to five stores, and I had read almost an entire book on my phone waiting for her.

But the worst was yet to come. Shopping, apparently,

was not all Bailey had in mind. Nope. Old Bails was after some girlie-type bonding. She felt bad that she had been absent all summer. And that she had taken Eli with her. A recognizable theme was beginning to develop with these two: guilt over leaving poor little Xandra Ryan, the most tragic person in the universe.

"I should have just insisted that my parents let me bring two people," Bailey said, not for the first time, as we looked at the menus at a café. We were at an outside table, and the lady next to us had a little dog in a stroller, and she was feeding him French fries. Bailey had just told me that her parents had only let her bring one friend, Eli, but now she felt horrible about it.

"Bailey, Eli is your *boy*friend. Of course you wanted to spend the summer with him. I completely understand — you should have zero guilt about this. Besides, it's not like I had this tragic summer or something."

"I know, I know, but I just feel really bad. There were some totally hot guys up there I could have fixed you up with, like that." Bailey snapped her fingers. A waiter standing nearby thought the finger-snap was for him and he hightailed it over to our table. "Miss?"

Bailey laughed at him. "Well, since you're here, I'll take another Pellegrino. X, you want another . . . was it a Coke?"

"Sure." I smiled at the waiter. Bailey knew it was a Coke. I always ordered Coke. Sometimes she just . . . I don't know. Maybe it was just that she actually drank Pellegrino.

"Anyway, what was I saying — oh, yeah. So many hot guys in the Hamptons this year. A lot of them were older, but that's not really a problem, is it?"

I literally had nothing to say to that. I hate saying fake things, but I heard myself saying, "I guess not," almost like a reflex, and then I hated myself more for saying it. Like I had ever dated an older guy.

"I know, right? So that would have been cool. It would have been really awesome if all four of us could have hung out."

"All four of who?" I couldn't stop myself from asking.

Bailey made a waving motion in the air between us. "Oh, you know, you would have met somebody there, like, for sure, and there are so many great things for couples to do there."

Curiouser and curiouser. Bailey's sudden interest in fixing me up was not only new, it was puzzling. Was she trying to assuage her own guilt — or Eli's?

"Anyway, you totally should have come," Bailey said, somehow skipping over and past the whole I-hadn't-been-invited issue. "Eli and I got really close there. Like I said, so many totally romantic spots. We stayed at this really old hotel, it's sort of like a B&B, except they totally leave you alone, if you know what I mean. No waking you up to take a walking tour or have breakfast with the owner or whatever. I mean, that's the worst, you know? So we slept really late there — well, we stayed *in* until really late." Bailey giggled, but didn't blush. But I got the idea.

I had a physical need to change the subject at that point, so I decided to just stand up. "I gotta pee," I told her. Bailey looked a little puzzled at my abrupt — and infantile — announcement, but she nodded, and I escaped.

I took a long time in the tiny bathroom, washed my hands twice, fixed my hair. But it was a one-holer, and somebody had already knocked twice, so I knew I had to give it up and go back. When I returned to the table, Bailey was playing with her empty bottle of fancy water.

"Sorry," I told her. "Too much Coke. Was your salad not good?" I asked, gesturing to her almost untouched plate.

"No, it's okay." Bailey frowned distractedly. "Listen, Xandra, I just wanted us to spend some time together." She was looking at me intently; usually Bailey was kind of distracted. "I really am sorry about this summer. Eli and I are . . . Well, I just should have either brought you along, or not taken him for so long . . . Just, please forgive me?"

Wow. I was beginning to feel like I had really underestimated Bailey. Even Eli, who had been my best friend forever, hadn't realized that when the two of them left for two months, they took my social life with them. It was pretty insightful and thoughtful of her to notice. It was too late to fix my summer, but still.

"Bailey, I am totally fine. I mean it. And thank you for, um, feeling bad. It's . . . nice of you."

"We're friends." Bailey smiled at me then. "Next time, you are coming, whether you want to or not. I will kidnap you," she said, grinning. "But . . . I did get you a present from there. I know we've been back forever, and I should have given this to you sooner, but you looked so sad, so I felt weird . . . Anyway, I thought you might like these." She handed me a fancy brown shopping bag with the top folded over, a hole punched through and tied with a bow. The bag had BEACH BAG written neatly in black Sharpie marker.

"What is this?"

"Just open it," Bailey said. "You're gonna laugh."

I opened the bag and I did have to laugh. It was one of those grab bags of remainder books they sell at little used bookstores. This one was full of slim Regency romances.

"Nice!" I told her. "I love these things. And I go through them so fast. These are really great, Bailey." I smiled at the title of one, *The Errant Earl*. "Thank you!" We hugged across the small table.

"You are so welcome. As soon as I saw that bookstore, I completely thought of you. That was the best day, too! That night, there was this party — I forgot to tell you about it. It was at Jason Ingram's. It went on for the entire weekend . . ."

Bailey gave me some more details about that weekend, and many others, but these details have been redacted from my brain. After the waiter brought our change back, we stood up at the same time, walked the few steps to the sidewalk, and Bailey hugged me good-bye. She was headed to meet Eli, I knew. I looked down at the bag in my hands. At least I had a used copy of *The Romantic Rogue* to keep me company.

CHAPTER FIFTEEN

THE FOOL CARD: YEP, THAT'S ME

"Use your intuition
It's all you've got"
— BROKEN BELLS, "THE MALL & MISERY"

Orlando, Florida — Saturday, October 30

"I wish I could have afforded to get some new cards. These are a disaster." I placed my old cards on the new table, next to the crystal ball.

"No, those are perfect," Lina said. "No one will pay if they see you using brand-new cards."

I blew an annoying stray lock of my hair out of my face for the hundredth time. "Well, that's a good thing, 'cause I am down to dust on the start-up money."

I looked around the mostly done room. Lina had taken me to the mall while the crew moved us to our current spot in Orlando. Hanging out with Lina definitely had its privileges. This time around, I'd spent load-in day shopping instead of shoveling.

We had bought purple and deep red silky material to hang in the entryway. Jamie had found a love seat somewhere. He didn't say much when he brought it. I had been a smidge frosty to him since Lina had seemed so weird about him. It was a nice cover for me, anyway — I had no idea how to relate to him after kissing him.

The seat was pretty old and pretty ugly, but I'd used a huge purple sheet to cover it and found a couple of embroidered pillows. So there was a little waiting area, and then the customers could come in to the reading room. The table Nick had brought was the centerpiece, draped with one of the scarves that had been his mom's. Add the crystal ball, my gargoyle lights, and some of the nicer half-price Halloween decorations Lina and I had found at Target, and the look was complete. I had run out of money before remembering candles, but Lina showed up with dozens of them, the tall white ones in jars like they use in churches. I didn't ask where they came from, just said thank you.

"Perfect," Lina said. She and I sat in the waiting area, in front of the love seat, and surveyed the finished product. We had lit the candles, and though it was still daytime, it was pretty dark inside. I had to admit, it looked good. I couldn't help smiling; I felt sort of proud of myself for putting it all together on such a teeny budget.

"Not too bad," I agreed.

"Are you kidding?" she asked. "Louie is so impressed, he wants to adopt you," she joked.

"I had a lot of help," I told her. "Most of it from you. Lina, I really don't know how to thank —"

"You don't need to," Lina cut me off, as she always did. "So, are you ready for tonight?"

Opening night. My stomach fell down near my toes. The setting-up was really more my area, I was afraid. I was much more likely to sign up to work backstage than to audition for a role. But all this was for nothing if I couldn't bring in customers and play my part.

"As ready as I'll ever be," I told her. "I just hope somebody shows up. And, if they do, I hope they don't laugh. Or ask for their money back. Or throw rotten tomatoes at me."

Lina moved to stand in front of me. "I know things are different where you're from, and you have some misconceptions about life outside the big city. But, Lexi, honey, I have to tell you, no one carries rotten tomatoes around with them."

I laughed a little then. "Well, that's one worry off the list, anyway."

I was sitting alone at the reading table in the trailer, shuffling my tarot cards over and over, trying to psych myself up for my debut, when Liska walked in.

"Lexi, would you do a reading for me?" she said. "It could be like practice, maybe?"

I tried not to show my surprise. "Have a seat." I waved my hand at the chair opposite mine. "How do you think everything looks?" I asked, then instantly regretted my choice of small talk. What if Liska wasn't impressed with the way the trailer had turned out? I trusted her to not lie to me — but I also trusted her opinion. Liska looked around slowly, not one to rush into anything. "I really like it," she told me, with an almost-smile. "You did a great job. In fact, this is much nicer than what Madame Tarus used to have. She relied on looking so much the part, I think."

"Thank you," I told her, meaning it. I shuffled the cards one more time and asked Liska to cut the deck. "So you have some questions in mind?"

She laughed. "One very big one, actually. But I thought I wasn't supposed to say . . ."

"No, you're right! I should probably remind people to think of a question, but not say it out loud."

Liska smiled. "See, it's good you're practicing on me." She paused. "Lexi, what will you study in school? When you go away to school?"

I paused in laying out her spread, surprised by her question. "I don't know if I'm going to get to go away to school," I told her. "I have to finish high school or get my GED first. And then there's the minor matter of how to pay for college. Your dad's being really great," I added, "but it's probably not going to be enough, not for a long time."

She nodded sadly. "I'm sorry. I guess your father would have sent you — would have paid for you to go?"

I nodded back and pushed my words past the sudden lump in my throat. "He would have," I told her. "I was gonna go to NYU, if I got in. But I'm not sure what I would want to study. Of course in college you can take a bunch of classes until you figure out what you're good at, or what you want to do."

Liska sighed. "That sounds amazing," she said. "I'd love to go."

"Wouldn't Louie send you?"

She shook her head. "He needs me and Lina and Eddie — needs our act. Without us, there isn't much left of the old circus. He couldn't stand it if all that was left was the carnival part — the games and the rides and stuff. It would kill him."

"But Louie must want you to be happy." I was upset for her now. Louie had kind of saved me, so I tended to think of him as Santa Claus. But it seemed that he was failing Liska in a big way. Of course, I had only met the Vranas at all because my own dad had failed me, though I felt like a bad daughter even thinking it.

"What about Lina?" I asked.

"Lina needs me to do the act; it's what we do. And she is happy here. She wants to stay here, with our father, with the circus. I couldn't leave," she said.

"But you came here with a question in your mind . . ." I trailed off, raising an eyebrow at her.

She grinned at me then. "Well, I didn't say the word *never*," she allowed.

I smiled back and finished laying out her cards, then turned over the first card: the Empress. I couldn't stop my reaction; I showed surprise. I was going to have to do better at this tonight — that was for sure.

"What does it mean?" Liska asked. "This first card sort of stands for me, right?"

I nodded. Madame Tarus must have done a reading for her at some point. "It does. The Empress, though, it usually means marriage, fertility. It's kind of a card of staying put." I couldn't help it; I frowned at her. This card didn't seem like a good answer to the question I thought she was asking.

Liska, though, was smiling. Kind of confusing, given that she had just revealed her desire to get the heck out of here.

"Lexi, I will give you a piece of advice," she told me, still smiling. "Don't assume you know what the question is. After all, how do you know the question I asked was about *me*?"

"Good point." I sat back in my chair and regarded her steadily for a moment. Then I leaned forward to uncover the rest of the cards. "Thanks," I added. "I've done readings for my friends or friends of my dad, but this is different. I don't know if I can pull this off."

"*I* know you will," Liska said, sounding so certain that I felt instantly better, more like a pro fortune teller than a girl with a deck of cards she bought with her birthday money at Barnes & Noble.

I flipped over the card in the second position. I explained to Liska that in the Celtic cross spread I was using, the second card is laid horizontally across the first card, because it represents obstacles for the questioner.

"The King of Pentacles — reversed," I read. Of course, I couldn't get an easy major arcana card to start. I closed my eyes for one moment — calling up the memory of the card's meaning — hopefully this technique would seem spiritual with my paying customers. "These court cards usually symbolize people," I told Liska. "It could be someone in your life, or some aspect of yourself. This King is . . . well, he's kind of greedy. The meaning of this card is someone who is very good with money. When the card's reversed, it's like the dark side of that trait." I looked at Liska, who was staring down at the card with concentration. "Does this sound like someone you know?"

Liska surprised me then by smiling. "Oh yeah."

"Okay, so that — or he — is the immediate obstacle to the question you were asking." I flipped the third card, positioned to the right of the first two: the distant past. The card came up the Ten of Wands. "This is a card about burdens — duties." I stopped myself from commenting on how apt this seemed, given Liska's life of work here at Europa. At her nod, I turned over the fourth card, the recent past. This one was the Wheel of Fortune, but reversed.

"Isn't that a very good symbol — the Wheel of Fortune?" Liska asked.

"It is, but when the card is reversed, the meaning changes. It stands for some sort of failure, an inability to meet challenges. When you look back at the previous two cards, there may be a pattern here. You may be trapped by circumstances, material concerns, or obligations — might need to face the challenge of breaking free from all that."

Liska still looked down at the cards, seeming to be lost in thought. I turned over the sixth card, the card of the immediate future: the Hanged Man.

"Ah, my old friend," I said to him. "I get this card a lot. You see how this little guy is hanging upside down, but he doesn't look hurt or anything? It's a card of suspension. But he can't stay there forever. The message here is that after a period of being in one place, having time to think, we need to act on what we have learned." Liska nodded again.

I turned over the seventh card. This position was about the questioner's state of mind. The card came up the Six of Pentacles. A rich man is trying to balance out his gold on a scale, and he just can't do it. There are beggars at the man's feet.

"This is an interesting card," I told Liska. "It's not so much about money as it is about balance. To find balance, this man has to give something away."

"Wow," Liska said.

"I take it this makes sense to you?" I smiled. I had a feeling it made sense to me, too. I thought I knew what Liska wanted to give away — her life on the trapeze. But would she? I kept the momentum up and turned over the eighth card: the Hermit. Another one of my old friends. "The Hermit is one of your external influences. It's a wise person, someone who will help you find what you are seeking."

Liska looked up from the table and into my eyes. "I think I know who that may be," she said slowly.

The ninth card came up the Page of Pentacles, reversed. The next-to-last position is about the person's hopes and fears. "When it's reversed, this card symbolizes a rebellious young person, someone who wastes — money, their time, or talents." Liska was nodding vigorously. "Okay, last card." I turned it over. "The Eight of Cups."

"That looks like a bad one," Liska said quietly. The card does look unpromising: A hunched figure turns away, setting off on a journey alone.

"This card does indicate a change," I told her. "It's about the end of something, which is sad, but it's also the beginning of something."

I sat back in my chair. Liska was still looking down at the table. After a few moments I asked her, "What do you think?"

"I think you are very talented. You'll do really well, but I knew that already."

"Thank you so much, Liska. Seriously. You don't just hand out praise, I can tell." I felt relieved to have gotten a good review. "But did you get an answer to your question?"

Liska nodded slowly. "I did. I think I did." I thought her eyes seemed suspiciously bright. "Lexi, thank you. For the reading."

We stood up. She hugged me across the tiny table, and with that she was gone.

I knew at that moment that I had made two new friends at the circus. I wondered if Liska would manage to break free from here. When I had been suspended, stuck, life had kicked me out into the street. I hoped that whatever got Liska in motion would hurt a lot less.

◆

That evening, Jamie helped get my iPod hooked up with the speakers. The other day he had come back with a RadioShack bag full of magical cords, so now I could control the music from inside. Another donation to my cause. I hated feeling like a charity case.

This thought strengthened my resolve to do well tonight. A few early customers were already coming down the midway, mostly families with kids in strollers, and some middle-school-aged kids.

"You have everything you need?" Jamie asked when we'd checked out the sound and experimented with the volume a couple times.

I tried to look confident. "Yep. Thanks, Jamie. For the love seat, too. That was really great of you."

"Least I could do," I thought I heard him mumble before he turned away.

How could Jamie possibly be this awkward with every girl he had kissed? Or maybe he usually confined his conquests to girls he was unlikely to ever see again, girls left behind at each circus town when we pulled up stakes and left.

I watched Jamie walk off, pushing away the confusion and awkwardness I felt about that situation. I had other confusing and awkward fish to fry. I ducked back into the trailer and scrolled through my iPod until I reached my give-me-ten-dollars-and-I'll-tell-you-your-future playlist.

I took my seat at the table and closed my eyes, listening to the first song, "Fortune Days" by The Glitch Mob. I shuffled the tarot cards, spreading them out before me. I was very glad I had spent so much time playing poker with Eli, because I at least knew how to shuffle really well. I selected a card by feel, pulled it out, and opened my eyes. The Fool: the beginning of a journey or adventure. That sounded about right.

"That's a good card," I heard a deep voice say, and I looked up, startled, into Nick Tarus's very dark eyes.

"The Fool?" I raised an eyebrow at him. Somehow I could talk to Nick without forgetting how to use nouns. I guess starting off being screamed at and insulted had sort of broken the ice with him, in a weird way. "It's a card about beginnings, I know that. But the name of the card isn't too complimentary. After all, the thing I'm the most worried about is whether or not anybody will want to have their future told by an unpleasant teenager."

"Ouch." Nick mock-winced. "That hurts. But you're an old soul — shows in your eyes. You'll be fine."

The way he said it, flat-out like that, no joking or irony, seemed almost to make it true. And then I snapped out of the spell *his* eyes had briefly put me under and felt nervous again. Who was I kidding?

"Practice on me," I heard him saying.

Had everyone in the whole circus decided I needed practice?

"But your mom is a professional," I told him.

"My *mother*, yes. But I never let her do a reading for me," he said as he expertly shuffled the cards. "So I really won't know any more about it than anyone coming in off the street. It will be the perfect unbiased opinion."

"You never let her?"

He narrowed his eyes slightly. "I don't actually claim to believe in any of this." He gestured to the cards and the crystal ball. "But my mother is quite insightful. Good at reading people. I was never anxious to volunteer to sit still and have her work her mojo on me."

"Well, you're safe as kittens with me." I reached over to take the now neatly shuffled and stacked cards from him.

"I'm not so sure about that." He smiled wickedly at me.

I tried to ignore that one. I laid out the cards, hoping I didn't blank on any of the divinatory meanings I had obsessively memorized for each of the seventy-eight cards — at least not in front of Nick. I turned over the first card, and I looked down to see a naked man and woman: the Lovers. Great.

"Attraction and temptation are indicated by this card." I tried to sound professional and avoid looking at him at the same time.

"Maybe there's something to this after all," he said under his breath, and then looked up at me. "Go on."

"We'll have to see what it means in the context of the other cards," I hedged, my heart beating so loudly, I was pretty sure he'd be able to hear it. What was wrong with me?

"Yeah, it seems like a really mysterious card." He grinned at me and leaned forward so that his right arm was touching mine. At least no other reading I could do tonight — or maybe ever — could be any more distracting. I quickly turned over the next card. I had already gotten the most embarrassing one, so I might as well keep going. I flipped over the Two of Swords, which shows a blindfolded woman kneeling, holding two crossed swords in the air.

"An impasse," I told him. "Whatever you are . . . asking about, there is an immediate obstacle or challenge to . . . finding the answer you are looking for." I snuck a look at him then, but he kept his face impassive. "It looks as though you're stuck in your own mind. You're deciding something."

Nick nodded slowly; the playful smile had faded, and he looked a little serious. "Sounds about right." He seemed to shake himself and remember that he was supposed to be encouraging me. "Go ahead, you're doing great. What does the next one say?"

I flipped over the third card, the one that was about the questioner's distant past. I was pretty curious about Nick's past myself; I wished I did know how to use these cards to pull some kind of answers out of him. But another part of me felt like that was a really bad idea.

"Uh-oh," I said to him, smiling a little. "The Queen of Cups, reversed. This is a card of dishonesty. May indicate an untrustworthy woman. Sounds like somebody in your past wasn't who you thought."

Nick nodded again, looking more interested. "As long as she's in the distant past, good deal. Keep going," he told me.

I guessed that was all I was getting there. I turned over the cards in the fourth and fifth positions, and both were from the Pentacles suite, more about material fortune than emotional, and both positive cards. The sixth card, indicating the immediate future, came up the Fool.

"Well, well. I wonder who that could be?" Nick grinned again at me. He took my hand in his and raised it to his lips, slowly. What was with this guy and hand-kissing? It was like he *knew* he was dealing with a girl who was addicted to Jane Austen or something. The little trailer got really warm then.

I finished the reading, but I have no idea what cards he got, or what I said about them. He kissed me again, on the top of my head, after he got up from the table.

"You will do very well tonight," he said softly, and then he was gone.

It took me maybe fifteen minutes to stop staring at the chair he'd abandoned and get up and move.

He was right about one thing. There was no doubt at all about who the Fool was.

CHAPTER SIXTEEN

IF ONLY

"It's about getting out of a rut, you need luck
But you're stuck and you don't know how"
— PET SHOP BOYS, "LOVE ETC."

---

13 Broome Street — Thursday, September 30

Okay, so I stopped posting status updates on Facebook a long time ago. I noticed that whenever someone posts something completely mundane and stupid, like *Sushi 2nite!* seventeen people have to comment on that. *I ♥ Sushi!* and *Spicy Tuna 4 meee!* But if you ever try to actually say something serious about your feelings or, like, your life, every one of your 386 "friends" is suddenly mute. So there you have it: My life is a post with no comments. Less interesting than spicy tuna.

I guess I could start a blog, but that would be like posting my diary online: no thank you. Plus, if no one has the time to respond to a seven-word status update, who, exactly, do I think would be reading some lame blog anyway?

It was only fifth period, and the day was already dragging. I was sitting on the floor, a little ways outside the caf.

All of a sudden, somebody's face was right in front of me. Bailey smiled at me tentatively, looking kind of concerned.

"You okay, X? You seem a little . . . I don't know. I guess just, are you okay?"

I nodded at her as she straightened back up, readjusting the strap of her black Balenciaga schoolbag. I only knew the brand name because I'd been with her when she'd bought it, and it cost just about the same as a month's rent on our apartment. I think I'd bought some gum on that outing.

"I'm just kind of tired, I guess," I told her. "But thanks for asking."

The thing about Bailey is, she has these bags and shoes that cost as much as the car my dad used to have, but she never makes fun of me for having the same bag since tenth grade, or the fact that it's from the Gap. When we first hung out, and I would admire something that was really expensive, sometimes she would try to buy it for me. After I said "no, but thank you" enough times she gave up, and she doesn't do it anymore, but that's the kind of person she is. I sometimes forget that when she's being sort of the Adventure Barbie Bailey. And then I feel like a crummy person.

"How're you doing today?" I asked her.

"Okay." Again, Bailey sounded kind of down-tempo. Usually she was more of an up-tempo girl. I wondered briefly if Bailey had a soundtrack in her head, too. Probably that was just me. Before I could think better of it, I asked, "Bailey, do you ever hear music in your head? You know, like even when there's none playing?"

She looked thoughtful for a second. "Sometimes, I guess. I sort of wish there were music playing all the time — you know, like on *The Real World* or something."

I laughed. "Exactly — that would be great. And if all the boring parts of my life would be edited out. Of course, that would make the Xandra show about as short as your average commercial break."

"Stop, loser." Bailey hit me on the arm. "You are always so self-depreciating, or whatever. I think you are totally interesting."

I smiled at her and through sheer force of will didn't tell her the word she wanted was *self-deprecating*. I fell in step with Bailey's long strides.

"If only life could be like it is on one of those shows," I said. "Everything's interesting and dramatic, and every argument is solved by them playing a song over the closing credits."

"Yeah, and they get to vent about everything in those confession boxes," Bailey said with a laugh.

"But actually, it would kind of suck for there to be cameras around all the time, ready to go when I did something stupid or embarrassing. Like most days."

She hit me again — and it hurt a little this time. "Hey, I told you to stop being so mean to my friend! You have to start being nice to yourself, X."

"Okay, I'll work on it," I grumbled at her, but I smiled, too. "But that would be really cool if . . ."

"Ohmygod, I have to go! I have, like, a million things to do before tonight!"

"What about period six?" I started to ask her, but she was already gone.

CHAPTER SEVENTEEN

CHEATING AT CARDS

"This is your blind spot, blind spot
It should be obvious, but it's not"
— THOM YORKE, "BLACK SWAN"

Orlando, Florida — Saturday, October 30

I sat across from my first paying customers — a couple dressed as pirates in honor of Halloween. The girl pirate was getting the reading, and she seemed a little unimpressed until her final card was the Star.

"This is a really positive card," I told her. "It's usually a sign of —"

"Ohmygod — I knew it! I'm so going to be in that movie! And then I'm outta here! I am *definitely* moving to LA now."

The boy pirate looked a little crushed, but she didn't seem to notice. I decided not to confuse her with the actual meaning of the card, and let her go away happy. (At least one of them was.) This was my first lesson in the customers seeing what they wanted to in the cards, and me not trying to stop them.

The rest of the first night went by in a blur of costumes.

It was hard to try to read people's faces when so many of them were wearing full-face makeup or masks, but I got through it. I had a line of people waiting right away. Luckily, I also started getting some help.

Nick came to check on me and found more people than I guess he'd expected, and then he stayed. He kept showing up each evening, helping me get set up, and then hanging around to sell the tickets and be my sort-of bouncer. I had only seriously needed his help one time so far — this guy who had been more interested in creeping me out than finding out about his future.

A couple of days after my debut, Nick was helping me light all the candles. I'd hit play on my iPod. I saved the special playlist for the customers; one of the hundreds I'd made last summer was playing. "Is this Radiohead?" he asked me.

"Thom Yorke," I answered, tilting a candle with a tiny wick to the side and trying to get the flame to grow. "He's the lead singer of Radiohead, though. Writes most of their songs. My dad saw him perform in the early nineties — he was in a band called Headless Chickens. I always loved that name."

"Reminds me of a circus geek," he said.

I cringed. "Aren't they supposed to bite the heads off live chickens? Have you ever seen one?"

"I can't actually say I have. You've seen the protestors

just for the animals that perform. There's no way anybody's going to bite the heads off animals in today's circus."

"Guess not," I told him. "This conversation took a strange turn."

"Don't look at me, music encyclopedia girl." He smiled and handed me his matches. "You've got fire now. By the way, in return for my awesome help tonight, I want you to make me a mix."

"Sure," I told him. He kissed me on the nose, and my heart jumped. "Break a leg," he said, and then went out to get the first customer of the night.

The lines stayed long all that week. As soon as it got late and the second show in the ring was over, there were mostly teenagers outside on the midway. That's when I got a pretty good crowd going outside the trailer. I had hung some lanterns out there and put candles in them, and with the music and the darkness, it was kind of clublike. It also didn't hurt that I now basically had a male model out there, drawing in all the girls.

One night, I gave readings for what seemed like about a hundred teenage girls, all dressed in what seemed the suburban Florida uniform for fall: a tight little sweater, itty-bitty denim skirt, and big furry boots. I did not understand the boots, because it was still over ninety degrees at eleven o'clock at night, but these girls were all set to tromp through at least a light dusting of snow.

I did my own share of sweating, trying to figure out each girl, see past the uniform. Tell her something she could maybe use, but not something she didn't want to hear. I concentrated on the tan, blond girl in front of me, trying to figure out what might be unique about her. Then I turned over her immediate obstacles card: the Death card.

The girl, whose name was Crystal, saw the card and promptly flipped out. "Really?! I'm gonna die — that's what that means, right? Oh my God!"

"That's not what it means," I told her. "I mean, it can actually be a really positive card. It can mean just the end of something —"

"*Oh my God!* The end of *my life*!" Crystal yelled. "Ashley! Get in here! Now!"

A girl who could have been Crystal's twin, at least as far as hair and clothes, ducked inside, Nick right behind her.

Crystal started crying, and Ashley glared at me. "I'm going to die!" Crystal sobbed. "This girl told me — she p-p-pulled this card, and it said . . . it said . . . *Death*!" She turned and saw Nick standing there and threw herself into his arms, sobbing, while Ashley continued to glare.

Nick patted her back and told her it was going to be okay, she wasn't going to die. I opened my mouth to finish explaining about the card, but Nick just shook his head at me. He led Crystal away, the angry Ashley in her wake.

A couple of minutes later, after I read for a cute little ninth-grade couple who held hands the whole time, Nick returned.

He threw himself into the seat opposite me. "God, that girl could cry." He pulled his now damp shirt away from his chest and made a face of disgust. "I thought she'd never stop. And then when she finally did, the other one started. I got them some Cokes and took them over to the Tower — told the guys to let them ride as many times as they wanted. Say, Lexi" — he leaned forward, raising his eyebrows at me — "you think we could maybe take the Death card out of rotation, hmm? I don't love the idea of being cried on for an hour every time you pull it."

"I didn't tell her she was going to die," I started to protest, but he put his hand up.

"I know what you're going to say — it can be a positive card, new beginnings and all. But maybe this crowd just isn't quite up to making that distinction?"

I shuffled the deck until I found the offending card, then I leaned forward and slipped it into the front pocket of his button-down shirt, patted the pocket, and smiled at him. He shook his head, stood up, and walked back toward his post, muttering something under his breath that I couldn't make out.

I got my cards and table ready for the next customer. Taking the Death card out was just more of what I had already been doing: cheating a little. I had pinched up the corner of my old friend the Lovers card, and I'd been reaching for it whenever it looked like it would really be appreciated. I mean, the card is about relationships, and we all have those.

I got a chance to advise one girl who kept hinting about a friendship — with a guy — that she wanted to turn into *more*. "Things will never be the same," I told her. "So just think really carefully before you leap."

"Is that in my cards?" the little blond girl asked. (I wondered if I should tell her to skip the Hurricane — she was exactly Jamie's type.)

I smiled, probably a little ruefully. "No, it's in my life," I told her. "And I wish it weren't. But everyone's different, every relationship. Either way, it won't hurt to consider things an extra time or two, right?"

She smiled back. "It's not like he sees me that way, anyway. So I've got plenty of time to think."

The next girl had her boyfriend in tow, this really beefy, loud guy, who was for some reason wearing a leather jacket in blatant disregard for the heat.

I turned over the Fool card and started to explain the meaning, but he started talking over me right away. "She's the fool," he said. "No doubt about it."

I tried to ignore him, but it wasn't easy. Basically it seemed like he was trying to get her to leave her family and move to Boston with him, and he tried to twist every card and interpretation to fit that end, even though from her face, the girl didn't want to do anything but stay right down here in the land of sunshine and furry boots.

"Hey, girlie," he finally said to me when I tried to tell his girlfriend that the Six of Cups meant happiness gained from family. "You obviously don't know anything. What are you, sixteen?" He was yelling by this point. "Who are you to tell us what to do? So why don't you shut up and give us our money back? How about that *interpetation*?" He said the last word wrong, without the *r*, and even though this jerk had just made every fear I'd had about this job come true, I still found it funny. Just as my very badly timed laughter was bubbling up, my bouncer appeared.

"Excuse me," Nick said from behind Jerky. "I think it's time for you to leave."

He smoothly reached around with a ten-dollar bill and put it in the front pocket of Jerky's jacket, which, now that I really looked, was made of cheap-looking vinyl. Jerky tried to grab Nick's hand, but Nick was faster and grabbed his instead, and from the looks of things was pretty much crushing it. I tried not to smile, reminding myself about karma.

Nick led the now loudly protesting Jerky out of the trailer, and his girlfriend turned around to mouth *I'm sorry* to me.

"Break up with him," I told her, taking momentary advantage of my de facto status as a fortune teller with a hot bouncer.

She smiled sadly, and I knew right away that she wouldn't. Why do people stay with jerks?

Nick put his head back in the tent. "You okay?"

I sighed. "I'm good," I told him. "Thank — really. I don't know what I would have done if you hadn't been here, though. But you can send in the next one."

Nick shook his head. "Louie ought to know better." He sounded angry. "As soon as I realized he planned to leave you alone, I knew I couldn't go yet."

With that, he went back out to manage the line. And I was left in a daze. He'd stayed for me? He was leaving the circus? Why did everyone have to leave? And why hadn't I seen this coming? He didn't work here. He had no attachment to me beyond a little speck of guilt that was now certainly assuaged.

Some freaking fortune teller.

$@#%!

*"We're like crystal
We break easy"*
— NEW ORDER, "CRYSTAL"

Orchard Street and Avenue A—Friday, October 1

I woke up in Eli's small bed, curled away from him, facing the wall, the wall I'd decorated long ago with a poster for the movie *The Brain That Wouldn't Die.* The woman with no body, bandages wrapped around her head and neck, and what looks like jumper cables attached to the sides of her neck, she was staring at me, and I felt stupid. And wrong, and bad . . . I looked at my watch. 5:34 A.M.

Eli was still sleeping, lying on his stomach, snoring quietly. It was freezing cold in his room. I sat up carefully; for some reason it was incredibly important not to wake him up — I didn't question the strength of this conviction, just followed it. I found my phone in the pocket of my skirt near the foot of the bed. I clicked the center button and was not all that surprised to see a blue box and nine missed calls. But I'd expected only my dad's number. Instead the most recent was an unknown 212 number. I switched to voice mail, my hand shaking, my stomach tightening. Who had called? Somehow, I knew, knew it was bad.

I heard a strange voice say something about an accident. My sharp intake of breath woke up Eli. He looked angry right away — Eli wasn't one of those people who took a long time to wake up.

"You need to get out of here. You need to get out of here *now*," he said, first thing, and his voice was that of a cold stranger.

He didn't need to tell me twice. I had to listen to the rest of the message, find out what it meant, and I had to do all of that somewhere else. I grabbed my skirt, my bag, opened the window, and stepped onto the freezing fire escape. Eli actually looked shocked, though I was following his directive; I was getting out *now*.

I stepped out, still in bare feet and without my skirt, and even went down the round metal stairs like that. I stood in the alley for one second, pulling on my skirt and boots, and then I just ran.

CHAPTER NINETEEN

MAKING SURE IT HURTS EVEN MORE LATER

"You left your door wide open, couldn't help but walk in
It's the last place I should be"
— SNOW PATROL, "ONE NIGHT IS NOT ENOUGH"

Boynton Beach, Florida — Sunday, November 14

It's really, really stupid, but sometimes I used to imagine something bad happening to me, and I'd imagine who would be upset about it. In tenth grade, when I had a crush on Miles Carson, I imagined that if I collapsed in bio class from some horrible disease (one that made you lose consciousness, but you still looked pretty, like a movie disease) that he might suddenly realize that he actually cared about me. He would run his fingers through his wavy, light brown hair and clench his jaw as he paced back and forth in the waiting room of the hospital. My dad would pat him on the back, and they would endure the waiting manfully together, until I was freed from my temporary bout of movie disease and we could go on a romantic date, maybe on his motorcycle, which would not mess up my hair.

After having such a stupid fantasy, of course, I would remind myself that not only had Miles called me Melissa once when he ran into me in the hall, but also that I knew exactly who would be in the waiting room if I ever actually did end up in the hospital, and that Eli and Dad were enough for me.

And then something horrible really did happen, and it was *really* horrible, worse than I'd ever imagined. Dad wasn't there, and Eli wasn't there, and I was completely and utterly alone.

The stupid girl who had those daydreams was so far gone, I couldn't even understand her. But in some ways, I still felt like her. I didn't want to be alone. I had friends now — Lina and Liska, who, along with Louie, were almost like family. But Nick was gone now, and even though my rational brain knew that it was stupid to want him here, it didn't change how I felt.

I was supposed to run the Fortune Trailer tonight . . . without Nick. At Nick's urging, Louie had loaned me one of the guys from the ring crew in case I needed backup. Nick wasn't happy with the selection — there was nobody available who really knew how to work the crowd, just setup guys. Nick told me that most problems are solved before the mark even comes inside. It was sort of cool how he called the customers *marks* — made me feel like a con man — well, con girl.

He said he hated to leave, but he had to get back to work. He was pretty vague about what work was, and I was too depressed to pester him about it.

Lina tried to make me feel better, telling me that Nick couldn't be my doorman forever. She told me that the little bit of money I was bringing in was nothing compared to what he would make in a night if *he* were the attraction. Didn't really make me feel better, actually.

The mysterious Nicolae Tarus was on everyone's mind while at Louie's Sunday dinner. Most everybody ate together in the cookhouse during setup and between gigs, and everybody ate a big lunch together on show days. But Sunday afternoon was family dinner at Louie's, a tradition his late wife had started. Ever since Lina had taken me in, I had been included.

We were all sitting around the table eating Liska's chicken casserole, and Louie was on a roll.

"Yes, it was good to have him back, though now he is gone again. His mother, though, her I do not miss!" He shook his head.

"Yeah, she likes to yell almost as much as you do." Lina snuck a look at her dad over the top of her iced-tea cup. Liska gave the most unladylike snort, the only ungraceful thing I'd ever seen — well, heard — her do.

"What do you mean?" Louie asked, sounding offended. "I am nothing like Reveka Tarus! She is hothead, and she has bad manners!"

"You have very nice manners, Daddy," Lina told him in a soothing voice. "But you do like to yell."

"Well, only when I have to. That woman, she yells to hear herself. I am glad she's gone. Lexi here is much more calm to have around, and she does just fine in the same job."

"I did just fine with *help*," I pointed out glumly. "Without Nick, who knows? Guess we're gonna find out."

"You'll do fine." Louie patted my hand, getting a little chicken gravy on it, which I wiped off surreptitiously under the table. I smiled bravely at him and hoped he was right.

I was determined to make a go of it on my own, or without Nick, at any rate. The crowds ended up smaller without him, and now I had a feel for the whole thing, so the first night passed uneventfully. Clay, the boy from the ring crew helping me, was skinny and blond, but he had a handsome face. He looked a little like an Abercrombie & Fitch boy who hadn't quite done enough reps at the gym yet, so he pulled in some female customers.

The first night without Nick turned into the second, and the third. On Wednesday, Louie let me open my attraction late so that I could watch the early show to see the Flying Vranas use the song I'd chosen, one by The Pierces. The ethereal-sounding song made their act seem very cool, kind of Cirque du Soleil. I was excited they had used my idea. Walking out of the tent that night, I felt a slight chill in the air — the first time I hadn't been hot since coming to Florida. I felt pretty good right at that moment, like I was part of things here. And I was saving money — slowly, granted, but I was. I could get my GED, and then I could go to college, get back on track. Though suddenly the thought of leaving made me incredibly sad. I hadn't wanted to come here, and now I didn't want to leave. Life was weird.

I had no idea at that moment how weird it was about to get.

I woke up at some point in the middle of the night. It sounded like someone was scratching at my window. I lay very still for a moment and waited for it to stop, hoping it would, but it just got louder, and then I heard, "Lex-i. It's me."

Who was "me"? I was pretty sure I didn't know anybody in this place who would either scratch on my window in the middle of the night or classify themselves as my "me."

I gave up the whole ignoring tactic, sat up, and shoved my feet into the flip-flops that were my new footwear staple. I looked down and decided my Arcade Fire T-shirt and pajama shorts were presentable enough for the middle of the night. I tried to look out the window, but the glass was pebbled and all I could tell was that my visitor seemed in fact to have a head. I tried to sneak out of the trailer quietly so I wouldn't wake up Lina.

Gracefully tripping out of the trailer and launching myself off the tiny steps were my next moves. And then I was in Nick Tarus's arms, my face inches from his.

"Hi," I said stupidly.

"Hi," he said, laughing. "Miss me?"

"A little," I managed, too breathless to be any wittier. "I thought you had to go back to work."

"I did go back to work. And now I'm back here to check on you. I kept having visions of you being chased out of town by an angry crowd."

As happy as I was to see him, my face fell — I could feel it. "You didn't think I could do it?"

Nick put me down beside him but kept his arms around my waist. "I *was* worried about you. But I also have faith in you. They're not mutually exclusive, you know."

For the first time since that day we'd met, it sounded a little, just then, like he was talking down to me.

"You're not here to stay, are you? Or to check on me. You're here to say good-bye, aren't you?" I had a tiny bit of trouble getting the words out, but I pushed through. Standing there with his hands still on my waist, his eyes looking into mine, I knew I was right, even though I didn't want to be.

He sighed, and I felt it travel through me, too. He lowered his eyes away from mine.

"I'm no good for you," he murmured.

"You are not that much older than me."

"It's not just about my age — or yours."

"You know how old I am?" I asked, distracted.

"I stole your wallet," he told me, pulling me a bit closer to him. "For a few minutes, anyway. Though it took longer to figure out your age than I thought — I was looking for a driver's license. Finally found some kind of ID card."

"I don't know how to drive," I admitted. "New York City girl — it costs a fortune to keep a car in New York."

"You should learn," he told me. "Now that you live out here in the middle of nowhere."

"But you're not going to teach me." I steered the conversation back toward the iceberg I knew was inevitable and just up ahead.

He shook his head. "I told you, it's not a good idea. For a lot of reasons. But I didn't want to just disappear without saying good-bye, not after . . ."

"It's not your fault, what happened to my dad," I told him, guessing what he was not saying.

"I know," he told me, reaching up and tucking a lock of my hair behind my ear. "I guess I have this problem staying away from you. You know" — he smiled a little — "I was ready to hate you when I first heard about you."

"I kind of got that from you yelling at me. But" — I looked up at him — "you still might . . ." My voice dropped to a whisper. "Hate me, I mean . . . It's a fine line . . ."

I saw the muscle in the side of his jaw tighten at that, and he stepped closer to me. "I couldn't hate you," he told me. "But I know what you are saying, Lexi. We should not . . . I will not . . ." He stepped away from me and started walking.

"Wait!" I didn't think, just called after him and started following.

He stopped. "I'm not leaving you right now — I'm just clearing my head. Come on." He grabbed my hand and led me toward the eerily quiet midway, where the abandoned rides lay waiting for tomorrow's crowd. He stepped up onto the carousel, and then picked me up with his hands on my waist. He sat me down in one of the small seats designed for parents riding with really little kids, then sat beside me, but not too close.

I was quiet for a moment, just watching him. I hated even such a small distance between us, but I felt frozen, afraid to move any closer. From the first time I saw him, basically right after we had stopped fighting, I had been pulled into his orbit, felt like I belonged there. But maybe he didn't feel the same way. He cared about me, felt sorry for me probably, but that was all.

I felt Nick take hold of my hand, and I found the guts to slide closer to him so that we were squashed together in the seat. My heart was racing and I think I forgot to breathe.

"Lex . . ." His voice was low in my ear. "You know I have to go. Aren't you kind of playing with fire here?"

"Yeah, well, I'm actually taking the advice of someone who does that for a living," I told him, turning my face to his. He let go of my hand and raised his to my face, tracing the line of my jaw with his finger. He leaned in closer and kissed me. We sat together on the silent ride for a long time. We didn't talk about his leaving anymore, but I felt the words hovering in the air between us. It didn't matter how close I sat next to him now. In the morning, I knew he would be gone.

CHAPTER TWENTY

SILENCE

112 Bowery — Friday, October 1

After the police station, and the morgue, I went home. I had heard all the details of the accident. I had smashed my phone to destroy the evidence of the frantic messages my dad had left me in the last minutes of his life, when he was wondering where I was, and also to destroy the messages from the NYPD.

It was all such a stupid waste. My dad was just crossing the street at the wrong time, and the cabbie was new, and he was lost, going the wrong way on a one-way street. They were both just trying to get home.

I let myself in with my key, but after that I had no idea what to do. I waited for someone to come and find me, to notice what had happened, but the sounds of cabs, horns, and sirens outside the apartment proved that life in the neighborhood was going on just like it had yesterday.

I wanted to call Eli and tell him what happened, but I

kept flashing back to the morning, and his face. The cold fire escape against my naked legs; the cold pavement and sharp gravel under my bare feet as I ran away.

I have no idea what happened to the rest of that day and night. My dad's lawyer came by the next morning and brought me to his office. After he broke the news to me — that I was broke — he gave me the TracFone he'd gotten me, a little black flip phone. He'd tried to call all night, and said he was worried I had lost my phone in all the confusion. He didn't know I didn't have anyone to call. But I took it and said thank you.

I put it in my pocket and walked the twelve blocks to Bailey's place. I didn't have a horribly painful memory of her face like I did with Eli. But as soon as she opened the door, I knew that she knew. I knew she hated me. Eli had felt guilty and unburdened himself, I guess. She slammed the door in my face.

It took only three more days to figure out that I had no place to live, no school to attend, and no money. I pawned the few things I could find in the apartment worth anything and started packing.

CHAPTER TWENTY-ONE

LADY THEO'S GOT NOTHING ON ME

"No, it's much better to face these kinds of things
With a sense of poise and rationality"
— PANIC! AT THE DISCO, "I WRITE SINS NOT TRAGEDIES"

Boca Raton, Florida—Friday, December 3

"Butter or kettle corn?" I asked Lina.

"Butter, definitely. But don't tell my dad or Liska," she warned. "Now that I'm grounded for a couple months, they'll be watching me like a hawk to make sure I don't get fat." She made a glum face, then turned her attention to the grocery store's impressive selection of potato chips.

"That sucks," I told her. "I guess flying through the air is kind of a job for the skinny. I never really thought about it."

"Yeah, try being on a diet for your entire life; you'll think about it more than you ever wanted." Lina smiled defiantly as she threw a bag of Cheetos into our grocery cart. I threw in another one for good measure. Nick was gone, and maybe never coming back. I planned to drown my sorrows in junk food.

Lina was bummed, too. She had gotten hurt the other

day — not a bad injury, but a sprain in her left arm. So we were on a quest for snacks. I was amazed and a little horrified at the Boca Raton version of a grocery store — the floors were marble, and about half the store was super-expensive organic food, European sodas, and cookies. It was like the Upper East Side only much, much bigger — and tanner and blonder. Lina and I skipped past all the designer produce and went straight for the good stuff. We were planning a movie night as soon as the show closed, but we already had enough for at least two of those in the cart.

When we got back to Europa with our five bags of junk, I got a surprise: Nick.

"I talked Louie into closing the Fortune Trailer," he said by way of hello.

Lina took half of the grocery bags from me, hit me in the stomach with them when I started to protest that she was hurt, and promptly disappeared.

"Well, hi to you, too, Nick Tarus," I said, blushing at the sight of him. "Glad you could drop by to get me fired, or whatever. I hope the ring crew is willing to take me back."

Nick grabbed the rest of the bags from me. I tried to fight him, but we were crushing the chips, so I let go. "I'm not trying to get you fired. Louie called me. I know what's been going on at this stop, Lexi."

Nick wasn't wrong. This was our last stop of the season, in what had turned out to be a rotten location. Boca was gorgeous, but the circus looked almost shabby here. Even though I'd felt like an outsider at the circus just a couple of months ago, now I felt like an outsider among the customers. Here, the parking lots were full of BMWs and Bentleys, and even the toddlers looked expensive.

The affluent teenagers who came out to spend a few bucks on the games, the rides, and the food looked like aliens to me now. Some of them came to hassle us, too — the guys hit on us girls in a way that made us feel dirty, and they kept trying to start fights with our guys. Jamie and the two Romanian brothers who worked on the ring crew had all showed up to breakfast the other morning sporting black eyes and looking proud of themselves. Louie made them wear makeup for the show, though, so that took some of the swagger out of them. And the crowds had been huge: college kids home on holiday break, the high school kids almost out of school, and everyone acting slightly crazy, drunk with freedom.

"But now you're back —" I began.

"I'm back because Louie called me to help him. I can't stay with you at the Trailer all night, so he's closing it. But don't worry, I got you a fun new job. You *and* Lina. I'll see you on the midway." Nick took the bags in, then reappeared a moment later, winked at me, and took off toward Louie's trailer.

It turns out it actually *was* a fun job.

"We get to run Go Fish tonight!" Lina squealed as soon as I opened the trailer door.

"Is that a good thing?" I asked.

"It'll be awesome! It's over by the Tower, so there's loud music all night, and I get to wear jeans!"

I could understand the attraction for her there. Her usual work uniform looked very binding and was full of poke-y sequins. "That's cool. But what *is* it?"

"You've seen it. It's in the little stand over by the funnel cakes. For two bucks you get three Ping-Pong balls, and you throw 'em and try to get one in a fishbowl."

"Doesn't that hurt the fish?"

"No, Lex. There's a trick to it. The ball doesn't hit the fish. And they're not playing for the live fish — we've got stuffed ones."

"Can we bring Coke and potato chips?" I asked her.

"Yeah we can! Now, go change into that black shirt with the scoopy neck. Nick will be hanging around that part of the midway for sure." She waggled her eyebrows at me and gave me a push toward my room.

Go Fish was much easier than telling fortunes. There was a giant trash can full of small-fish prizes, and we gave away probably more than we should — every cute kid who came our way left with a fish, whether their dad or mom showed any ring-throwing skill or not.

Between the holiday mood that the carnivalgoers had brought with them — on vacation, or about to be, from school or work — and us being away from our "real" jobs at the circus, Lina and I were giddy and punchy. Craig, the ride operator for the nearby Tower, was blasting classic rock, and

Lina and I sang along to songs by Blue Öyster Cult, Styx, Kansas, the Eagles, and Lynyrd Skynyrd. Somehow we managed to gather a little crowd as we sang along to Journey's "Separate Ways." I caught Nick's eye from a distance; he was watching me, but I kept right on singing. He looked younger than he usually did tonight, dressed in a black T-shirt and holey jeans.

We were singing the chorus — "Someday love will find you, break those chains that bind you" — and really selling it when I saw him standing there in the crowd.

Eli.

I know I stopped singing, and something of what I felt must have shown on my face, because I saw Nick take a step forward. The world looked impossibly bright for one instant, and then everything went completely dark.

I came to with my head in Nick Tarus's lap, Lina's concerned face a few inches from mine. We were on the floor behind the wooden box that enclosed the game, and I couldn't see past the edge of it to see if Eli was still there, or if he ever had been. It seemed like I'd imagined him. But another part of me knew I hadn't — the shock of seeing Eli appear in this world had to be what knocked me out. I wasn't a fainter — in fact, I had been pretty sure a few minutes ago that I would successfully navigate my entire life *without* fainting like an idiot. I hadn't fainted when they'd told me about my dad, even.

I heard the ominous opening chords of Hendrix's "All

Along the Watchtower" and struggled to sit up, determined not to act like a stupid fainty girl for one more second. But I sat up too fast and heard Nick say, "Whoa, slow down."

"I'm fine," I told him, but he was still holding me.

"Lexi, what happened?" Lina asked, her delicate features contracted in concern.

"Stay put, Lex," Nick said as I struggled against his arms. For some reason, it seemed really important that I get to my feet.

"Let her go," I heard a familiar voice say, though the tone of it was unfamiliar. He was trying to sound macho, which was new, and would be amusing if I hadn't just passed out. And in front of two of the three guys I had seriously made out with in my life. Now if Jamie were here, I thought wryly, my humiliation would be complete.

"Jamie, go get Louie," I heard Lina say one second later. Of course.

"I mean it, let her go." Eli, who Nick seemed to have utterly ignored, tried again, stepping even closer to the edge of the box and leaning over.

Without a word, Nick scooped me up, hoisted me in his arms, and carried me out of the game box, Lina scurrying ahead of him and opening the back swing-door as though they'd choreographed it. Ha! Take that, Eli. It was almost worth fainting, that look on his face as he saw Nick pick me up.

"Have a couple of the guys . . . detain . . . that boy," I heard Nick tell Lina, who nodded and disappeared.

For the first time in my life, I had been rescued, just like in one of those ridiculous Regency novels. The only trouble was, I was pretty sure that when Nick found out why the sight of my former best friend made me pass out, he wasn't going to be too interested in saving me anymore.

Eli followed us to Louie's trailer, where Louie was waiting for us, wringing his hands and asking Nick if he needed to call a doctor. He was still wearing his ringmaster gear, minus the hat, but he looked pretty funny dancing around Nick, who put me down on the couch in the trailer.

"I'm okay!" I protested.

"What happened?" Louie asked Nick.

Nick looked down at me, narrowing his eyes. "She fainted. She saw someone who apparently she did *not* want to see. Someone I'm going to go take care of right now."

"Wait!" I yelled after him, but he was already out the door.

I got to my feet and was headed for the door as I heard a strange replay of my first conversation with Nick.

"Who the hell are you?" he was demanding of Eli. Emerging out onto the rickety trailer steps, I could see for myself that Eli was backing away slowly; he looked so young and skinny next to Nick.

"No, who the hell are *you*?" Eli asked belligerently, in spite of the fact that he was still backing away. I saw his chin go up a little like it did when he was deciding to be defiant.

I started to walk toward them, meaning to step between them, when Lina tugged my arm back.

"Don't ever get in between two guys who are about to fight, Lexi. I learned that the hard way once."

"But I think they're about to fight about me!" I squeaked.

"We're not going to let them fight," I heard Louie say behind me. "Just don't you go stepping in between 'em."

"Xandra!" Eli sounded upset, and a little confused.

Nick shot me a strange look with a question in it.

I sighed. Talking to Eli was not something I felt like doing ever again. But it didn't seem like he was going to leave.

"Let me talk to him, okay?" I said to Nick. "For, like, a minute," I added, giving Eli a dark look. Nick took a step forward, but I put my hand up to stop him. "I'll be fine," I told him. "I was just . . . surprised to see him. I'm fine. It's all fine."

"Yes, because fainting and then obsessively repeating the word *fine* is so very reassuring," Nick said dryly as I walked past him, back toward the trailer. I didn't look to see if Eli followed me — I figured he had. If he was going to give up easily, he'd had his chance at that anytime in the last half hour.

I walked back up the stairs of the trailer, sat down on the couch, crossed my arms, and waited. Eli came in a few seconds later, and I saw him pull the door shut. And then I was looking at Eli, whose face I never thought I'd see again. I was transported back to two months ago, when all I had wanted was someone to be there for me. And the one person who I'd thought always would be had left me completely alone on the day my father died.

"Why are you here, Eli?" My voice sounded cold even to my own ears.

"I came to find you." He stood in front of me, his hands in the pockets of his jeans and his head down. "It wasn't easy . . . No one knew where you'd gone. I finally tracked down your dad's lawyer . . . He . . . helped me."

"Great." I sat back so I could look up at him. "Speaking of my dad. He died, Eli. He *died*, and you didn't come to the funeral. Or check on me, or give a damn about me then. So I guess I'm back to the original question. Why are you here? What could you possibly have to say to me now?"

"I came to apologize, X. I know . . . what I did. I know — but, look, it was complicated —"

"No, it wasn't, Eli. It was simple. He died. In the street, like a stray dog. With no one to claim him, because I was off *fooling around* with you." I snarled the last. "And then when they finally found me, it was just in time for me to get kicked out of the apartment, kicked out of school, and have just enough money after selling my dad's records to buy a bus ticket out of there. So it's all really pretty simple. While you went back to your beloved girlfriend, I figured out, all alone, what to do with my dad's body. And then I figured out how to not starve to death myself. So, yeah. Thanks for the apology, but I don't really need it anymore. That time has passed — it's over. It's all over. You and me, we're definitely over."

And suddenly I just wanted to be out of that trailer. Eli was staring at me with what looked maybe like tears in his eyes, and I didn't want to see them fall, didn't want to feel bad for him, didn't want to go back there. So I ran.

I didn't get far; Nick caught me and picked me up again — it was getting to be some crazy romance novel habit of his. He carried me away from Eli and from two months ago, and I let him.

He put me in his car, and we drove for a while. "I won't ask you about that kid," Nick said as we drove. "But if you want me to get rid of him for you, I will."

The way he said it, he sounded so serious — like he was a mobster offering to off somebody for me. I giggled, but then it sort of turned into a sob.

"I'm sorry!" I told him, forcing myself to stop cry-laughing. "You don't have to get rid of him. I mean, he'll probably go on his own. It's just . . . he used to be my best friend. And I haven't seen him since that night . . . when my dad . . ." I swallowed hard. I couldn't finish.

"You don't have to tell me anything." Nick looked over at me, then reached out and found my knee and squeezed it. "It will all be okay."

"Feels like it now," I told him. *With you here* was the part I didn't say out loud. I remembered Lina telling me about how Nick always took care of everybody. "I'm sorry I fainted like an idiot," I told him.

"You aren't an idiot. I think you're actually pretty brave. You came here all alone, you've handled everything Louie's thrown at you. You never even cried, unless you count the time some jerk yelled at you." I looked over at him and saw him smile in the dark. "And you make the best mix CDs," he added.

I had finally worked up the courage to give it to him right before he left. I'd obsessed over that mix more than any one I'd ever made. I turned a little away from him to hide a giant smile. I was an emotional yo-yo tonight. "You liked it?"

He reached over and turned up the volume, and I could hear that he had it playing in the car. We listened and drove for a long time. The CD started over, but he kept on driving.

CHAPTER TWENTY-TWO

HAPPY FREAKING HOLIDAYS

"You're the last thing I wanna see underneath the tree
Merry Christmas, I could care less"
— FALL OUT BOY, "YULE SHOOT YOUR EYE OUT"

Frostproof, Florida—Saturday, December 18

So Eli Katz works at my circus now. Whatever.

It's some sort of self-imposed penance. It's the stupidest thing I've ever heard of in the entire history of the world.

But it turns out Louie really does have a soft spot for strays — not just me — and he gave him a job. We're not even open; we're in winter quarters, for God's sake, and he gives Eli a job. Eli, who can't even open soup cans properly — this is who Louie has helping Jamie do preventative maintenance on the rides. Good luck not dying, townie children.

So Eli is here, and he stopped trying to talk to me, finally, but there isn't much reason for him to be here if you don't count me. It's probably winter break from school, but he doesn't show signs of budging. Unless he randomly decided to forgo senior year at Sheldon and applying to Columbia in favor of carrying Jamie's tools, because that would definitely make sense.

Everyone else who I actually *wanted* to be here was gone. Lina and Liska were visiting their aunt in Michigan, and Nick had gone off to Miami to check on some apartment building he owned. The fact that he owned actual real estate seemed to separate him even further from a person such as myself whose worldly goods would fit inside a decent-size duffel bag.

The weather finally turned almost cold. It was nothing even approaching October-in-New York cold, but it felt more like winter. We were parked in the whimsically named town of Frostproof. There was nothing there, and, if there were, I would need a car to get to it. Liska had surprised me with a GED study book, but it seemed pretty cake-y after my year of hard time in math and more math, since that was the only class I'd ever really struggled with.

The combination of boredom and Eli being around was really reminding me of last summer, which was the exact last thing I wanted. So for the second time in as many months, I decided to run away from home.

One hundred and eighty-six miles away there was a city — not New York, but an honest-to-God city. And suddenly I knew I had to go there. I wasn't going to let not knowing how to drive, or not having a car, stop me.

He looked pretty surprised to find me knocking on his door. I tried to smile my most charming smile.

"What do you want?" Jamie asked, sounding kind of surly. He ran his hand through the back of his wet hair; it seemed he'd just gotten out of the shower.

"Hey to you, too." I frowned. "I need a sort of favor . . ."

"My foot's still throbbing from the last Lexi-related favor." He gestured down to his foot, which was black, blue, purple, and a little yellow all around his toes and up the middle.

"Eli was *not* a Lexi-related favor. I tried to tell Louie to make him go home. I don't want him here. I have no idea what he's even still doing here. In fact, let's pick a new winter spot and leave him here." So much for my being charming.

Jamie seemed to thaw fractionally. "That guy is so annoying. No wonder you left him."

I didn't point out the extreme lack of accuracy of that statement, nor did I go into the many compelling reasons I had left New York. I only nodded my head in agreement and looked sympathetically down at his foot.

"So what did he do?" I asked.

"Dropped a wrench on it," Jamie said, and then cursed in some language I couldn't recognize and hadn't known Jamie spoke. But I could figure out that he wasn't saying anything too great about old Eli.

This made me smile, and Jamie almost smiled in return. "So, you said something about a favor?" he prompted.

I nodded. "Teach me to drive?" I asked him.

"You don't know how to drive?" Jamie asked, his tone sounding as though he were asking something more like *You don't know how to convert oxygen into carbon dioxide?*

"No," I told him. "Remember how I told you that nobody drives in New York?"

"But how do you go anywhere?"

"Subway. Bus. Taxi. Walking — mostly walking."

"Wow." He shook his head, probably thinking how long a walk it would be from here to . . . anywhere.

"But if I'm going to live here, I really do need to know how to drive," I told him. "I really, really want to learn. And I promise not to kill your car," I told him.

Jamie was shaking his head back and forth very emphatically, and my heart sank: He was going to say no.

"Not my car," he said. "Mine's a stick. But I think I know whose car we can borrow."

"Eli came in a car?" I asked, mystified now myself as I followed Jamie out to where a few cars were parked. "I knew he could drive, but I didn't know he had a car . . ."

"I don't think it's his," Jamie said. "Not sure whose it is. It's about a hundred years old, though, so who knows how fast it'll go. But should be good to learn on. And from what I hear, the dude owes you." I didn't comment on that, but saved the knowledge that Eli had unburdened himself to Jamie.

Jamie used the key he mysteriously had in his pocket

(I didn't ask), opened the passenger-side door, and got in. I surveyed the old compact car for a moment: It was a sort of dull grayish color, and I wouldn't have had any clue what kind of car it was, but the back said *yota Ca r* , so I was guessing it was a Toyota Camry. I got in the driver's seat beside Jamie, putting my backpack between the two front seats.

Jamie put the key in the ignition. I was a little surprised when the engine immediately roared to life. "Runs pretty well," Jamie observed. "I drove it down the 630 a ways, ran real good. Okay, now." He sat back in his seat and put his hands flat on his lap, maybe restraining himself from doing any more of the driver's side jobs. "Go ahead and put your seat belt on, then get ready to pull out of here."

I put on the seat belt, no problem, but the "pull out of here" thing was a whole other story. "Don't you want to explain it to me first?" I asked. "I mean, give me a lesson?"

I heard him sigh a very small sigh, but he smiled and spoke patiently enough. "This *is* the lesson, Lexi. It's kind of a hands-on thing. Just put your hands on the wheel, three and nine o'clock. Good. Now put your right foot on the brake."

"Which one's the brake?"

"Wow — square one. Okay, the one on the left, the one that's longer across than up and down."

"Where does my left foot go?"

There came the sigh again. "Your left foot goes nowhere," he told me.

My look of confusion must have been pretty intense, because he barked a laugh. "You don't have to shove it out the window, just don't drive with it. Put it up on that little, like, shelf over there, get your whole left leg out of the way."

"I thought people used two feet to drive. I feel like I've seen that."

"Stick shift," Jamie said on a yawn, so it sounded more like *rick lift*. He leaned his head back against the seat and closed his eyes for a second. His bright blue eyes opened and fixed on mine. "You are really going to owe me for this one," he said.

"I know." I smiled. I tried to breeze past the sudden flashback of my one night playing the role of the townie girl Jamie made out with behind the midway. "Okay, so what now?"

"Now you drive. No putting it off any longer. Put your foot on the brake, put the car in gear, move your foot to the gas — gently — and let's go."

I fumbled and got the gearshift out of *P* and into *D*, then moved my foot super cautiously from the left pedal to the right one. It didn't seem to be working, so I put more of my weight on the right-hand pedal, and the car lurched forward. But Jamie didn't yell at me, just gritted his teeth, from what I could see out of the corner of my eye. We had been parked in the grass, so I tried to steer toward the partially paved path that led out toward the road.

The field where the show was parked for the winter was

off of a quiet two-lane country road. I remembered that it was kind of to the right, so I began to take that path, but Jamie broke in and asked me why I was driving into the woods, so I turned the wheel the other direction.

I practiced stopping and turning. We went out onto the main road and I pushed the accelerator down until the speedometer said sixty.

"I think you've got the hang of it," Jamie observed, laying his head back against the seat again and yawning once more.

"When do you have to be back to work?" I asked him.

"March 1," he said, opening one eye slowly, like a big blond owl. "I've put the rides to bed. I was basically hanging out."

"Do you mind if we keep going?" I asked him.

He crossed his arms and settled down further into the seat like he was settling in for a nap. "You could use the practice," he said on one last yawn. "Go for it."

"You don't care where we're going?" I asked him.

He answered without opening his eyes. "Since I'm pretty sure you're going wherever Nick Tarus went, I'm guessing Miami."

"Wow," I breathed. "Maybe you should be the fortune teller."

"That's what I keep telling everyone," he said, and then he fell asleep. I found Route 27 south and sat back to enjoy my new driving skill.

And I didn't feel bad at all about stealing Eli's car.

Driving was awesome. On the quiet two-lane highway, we passed other cars only occasionally. The road was pretty much flat and straight, and I tried to keep my speed steady at around sixty miles an hour. The cars that came up behind me always passed me, and I didn't mind. Sixty felt like flying. We passed a huge lake on the right, drove over a long bridge, and I got a sudden rush of what felt like freedom. I was somewhere I'd never been before, driving past houses with people in them I'd never meet. The world seemed so big and full of possibilities.

I couldn't believe I'd driven so far basically alone, because Jamie had slept through the whole thing. I was feeling pretty proud of myself when I pulled over at a gas station. According to the signs I'd been following, Miami was less than thirty miles away.

My first act as a responsible unlicensed driver was putting the car in park and taking the keys out of the ignition.

My second act was to scream and use my backpack to assault the stowaway in the backseat.

What I had taken to be a bunch of Eli's stuff under a blanket in the backseat had been *Eli* asleep in the backseat.

That's right: The first time I did something even remotely illegal — stole a car — it wasn't actually stealing, because the owner was in the freaking backseat the whole time. At least I'd still driven without a license.

"Hey! Xan, stop! It's me."

"I don't know if you've been paying attention these last few weeks, but *it's me* isn't exactly something that's gonna make me stop hitting you," I told him and wound up my bag for another swing. Jamie caught it, though, and, looking none too pleased to have been woken up, said simply, "Hey, cut it out, you two."

I didn't like the way Jamie said *you two*, like, *Oh, you two — isn't it cute how you're play-fighting now, but we all know it's giggles and hugs in your future? Ha!*

It was also kind of weird that Jamie didn't seem surprised that there were two people in the car with him now.

"Thanks, bro," Eli said, looking smugly at me now that his ride-fixing buddy had spoken up for him.

"Shut up back there. I haven't forgiven you yet for crushing my foot." Jamie put his head between the two front seats to look back at Eli. "And you should never say *bro*."

I giggled, then realized that in giggling I was pretty much fulfilling the tacit prophecy Jamie had made. My days of giggling with Eli were over.

"Sorry, dude," Eli muttered quietly.

Jamie was back in arms-crossed, eyes-closed mode. "Yeah, you should also avoid *dude*."

I had to really work on not giggling at that one, but with Jamie at least feigning sleep, I finally had to look at/ deal with Eli. And the ironic thing was, I had given him this captive audience opportunity, just like I'd gift wrapped it for him. We were somewhere outside Miami where I didn't know anyone and I was in Eli's car. As angry as I was at him, I wasn't about to leave him by the side of the road in South Florida. I kind of wanted to, but I wasn't going to.

I looked over at Jamie; he was looking to be no further help for a while. So I took the one tack I knew would both please Jamie and unnerve Eli. Unfortunately, flirting is like a foreign language to me. But I resolved to give it a whirl anyway.

I leaned over Jamie to open the glove compartment, leaning a little more than was strictly necessary. I heard a sharp intake of breath from the stowaway in the backseat and knew my evil plan was working. Jamie's eyes opened to slits, but there was a familiar light in them. "Whatcha doin' down there, little Lexi?"

I summoned the spirit of the most vacuous and skilled flirt in my class at Sheldon, Ashley Smart. "Looking for a map." I glanced up from under my lashes. "I'm lost," I told him ruefully.

"Are we still on 27?" he asked, confused.

"We're still on 27," said a flat voice out of the backseat.

"Then we're not lost."

"Really? That's awesome! I'm so glad you're awake, though, Jamie. I wouldn't want to try to drive the rest of the way into Miami all by myself."

"What am I, chopped liver?" came the voice from the back.

"Dude, did you really just say that? It's like you're eighty." Jamie shot Eli a look.

I was really starting to adore Jamie.

I got out of the car and started to grab the gas pump, but Eli was right behind me, muttering that he would do it. Eli pumped and paid for the gas, then climbed back into the backseat.

"I'll drive," Jamie said abruptly, unstrapping his seat belt and getting out. He was opening my door in another couple of seconds. I shrugged and walked around the front of the car to get back in the passenger side.

"So why were you lurking in the backseat this whole time, exactly?" I decided to forgo my not-talking-to-Eli resolution for the moment, at least.

"It's my car," Eli snapped. I looked back at him, but his face was already apologizing — I guess it took him a second to remember that he was actually trying to get back into my good graces. "I mean, I was sleeping in the backseat of *my car*. It's where I sleep these days. I didn't stow away or anything. You guys hijacked my apartment."

"Since when do you have a car?" I asked him.

"Since I used my college money to buy one."

"How did you get around Stan on that one?" I asked. Nothing was more important to Eli's dad than college.

"He's not really speaking to me right now — so, I guess I didn't. The money was in my account, and I used it without asking. And my mom is on his team, so you have a lot of company in the not-talking-to-me club."

"Oh God, dra-ma, *enough* already." Jamie sat up and switched on the radio. "Why don't you two make up or whatever when we get to Miami, yeah? I'd rather not actually turn into a girl before we get there, if it's all the same to you."

He was trying to flip through the stations, but he was making me nervous, so I took over. I snuck a look back at Eli. He had taken Jamie's directive seriously, apparently, because he was sitting back all the way behind Jamie's seat, his face turned toward the window. I tried to flip past a station playing "Jingle Bell Rock" by Hall & Oates, but Jamie called out, "Hey! Leave that one! I like it," and began to sing, loud and completely off key.

Yeah. It's the most wonderful time of the year.

Almost an hour's worth of holiday favorites later, Jamie pulled the car into a pink roadside motel. It was one of those strip hotels, with all the rooms and doors facing the road and a big square pool in the parking lot. Because nothing says relaxation like swimming in a parking lot. "Seriously?" I asked him.

"How much money you got?" he asked me. "Seriously?"

Good point. "I mean, awesome!" I faux-chirped.

"I'll stay in the car," said the martyr in the backseat.

"I wouldn't do that here, dude," Jamie told him. "You can stay with us."

"He is not!" I glared at Eli.

"I didn't ask to!" Eli glared back.

"Aw, Mom and Dad, don't fight — it's Christmas!" Jamie said in a mock little-boy voice, which struck me funnier than anything had since the return of Eli, and I laughed.

"That's the spirit!" Jamie cuffed me on the shoulder. He handed me twenty-one dollars and said, "Here's my contribution. I'll be in the pool."

"It's December," I called after him.

"It's heated," he threw back over his shoulder. I shrugged and started toward the office. I walked forward a few paces, then stopped, remembering what Eli had said about Jamie and me hijacking his "apartment" — how he'd been sleeping in his car. "You coming?" I turned around to holler at him.

Eli scrambled out and ran to catch up. I wondered how long this strange guilt-based power would last.

We checked into a room with two double beds and got a foldaway cot, which of course martyr-boy piped up that he would take. Eli actually paid for the room, wouldn't take Jamie's or my cash, then grabbed the key from the front desk guy and walked a little ahead of me to unlock the door.

"Do me one favor," he said, pausing with his hand on the door handle, his eyes on the door. "Please."

I waited for him to say more, but then when it didn't seem like he was going to speak, I reluctantly said, "Okay . . ."

"Just hear me out, X? I know what I did is . . . I know you can't forgive me. But I still need to tell you . . . I came a long way, and I've been waiting . . . Please, will you hear me out? Today?"

I nodded, but he wasn't looking at me, so I spoke, though my voice sounded strange. "Okay," I said again.

I followed him into the hotel room. The bedspreads had seascapes with seagulls all over them. Classy.

I took the bed farthest from the door and threw my bag onto it. I sat on the side, pulled my legs up Indian-style, and waited.

"Whew, okay. This is harder than I thought." Eli paced in the small carpeted area in front of the two beds.

"Maybe you should sit, too." I was surprised to hear myself helping him, but he looked a little bit like he was going to hurl, and I couldn't help it.

"Good idea." Eli took my advice and sat on the side of the other bed, but he didn't relax; it was really more leaning than sitting. "Thanks," he added, and took a deep breath. "So, the thing is, I came to find you because I had to tell you how sorry I am. I know I'm too late, and I know I can't ever make up for what I said, and did . . ." He drew a ragged breath. His eyes looked bright, as though he might cry. "So I need to tell you I'm sorry about that. Sorry that I was so cold, that I said what I said, that I didn't run after you, that I was such a coward . . . all of it."

I didn't look back up at him. I couldn't. It had been so nice to live in a world in which I could at least try to forget that horrible morning, where no one knew about it or remembered it. Eli showing back up had put an end to all that marvelous pretending. There was a loose thread on the seagull bedspread, and I pulled it, wrapping the thread tight around my index finger, cutting off the circulation.

"And then you told Bailey," I heard myself say in a very small voice.

"Yes," he admitted softly.

"Why?"

He drew another ragged breath. "I don't know if it matters now. I don't know if you'll believe me. I broke up with her. I told her about us because I knew I could never go back to her, not after what I — we — had done. I wanted to come back to you with a clear conscience. But then you were gone."

"Of course I was gone!" My voice wasn't so small anymore. "My father *died*. And you were so worried about hurting Bailey that you left me to deal with that *alone*, Eli. Completely and totally alone."

"X, I didn't know about Gavin," he said very quietly. He stood up and began to pace again. "I went to Bailey, I told her what we had done; I ended things. And then I went after you. I knew it was too late, but I had no idea then how late. You weren't home; I left you messages — a hundred messages. And then I went to school on Monday and you weren't there. I figured you didn't want to talk to me. Nobody knew about your dad. I mean, I guess Dr. Cranston did, but she didn't make an announcement or anything. I went by your place Monday night and saw you; I stood down in the street and looked up and saw your light on, and I saw you walk by the window. I wish I'd just gone up, right then . . . if only I'd known. But I couldn't — after what I'd said — and you were still ignoring my phone calls. I thought maybe I owed you some time . . ."

"I smashed my phone," I whispered.

Eli sat back down right across from me. "I figured something like that, later. On October 12, I stopped getting your voice mail and started getting 'This number is no longer in service,'" he explained. "That Wednesday afternoon, I heard about your dad at school. I don't even know who told me. I left as soon as I heard it, ran all the way to your place. But you were already gone."

Neither of us spoke for a long moment and the silence grew between us. Suddenly Eli knelt on the carpet between the two beds at my feet. "I understand that you can't ever forgive me for the way I acted, or for leaving you alone. But I needed you to know the rest, at least. That if I had known about your dad, that I would never, *never* have stayed away."

I pulled hard on the loose thread, making a giant snag. "That's not what I thought," I said carefully, and was surprised to find out I was crying. I wiped my eyes with the back of my hand. "That's not what it felt like."

"I know, X . . . Lexi . . . I know." He pulled me to him, off the bed, and down onto the floor with him, into his arms. I went stiff at first, and then something unbent — or broke — in me. My best friend hadn't completely abandoned me. Eli hugged me, hard, one large hand on the back of my head, pulling me to him.

And that's how Jamie found us. "Aw, I knew you two

crazy kids would make up," he said, rubbing his pool-wet hair with a towel.

I extricated myself from my damp embrace with Eli. He sat back, his eyes on my face.

Looking for a distraction, I glanced back at Jamie, who was just wearing a towel.

"Um, Jamie. What did you wear to go swimming?" I asked him.

"Wear?" He actually sounded confused. "Just gimme a second to put on some pants and then let's grab dinner. I'm starving."

Eli stood up and extended a hand to me, then hoisted me up beside him.

"Thank you for listening," he said softly. "If you want me to go now, I will."

"Do you want to go?" I asked. "I mean, you should go. Back to your real life."

"You were my real life," he said, leaning close to me. "As long as you're speaking to me, I'm not going anywhere."

"Come *on*," Jamie said from the doorway. So the three of us went to Arby's for dinner.

CHAPTER TWENTY-THREE

Surprise

"You don't want to hurt me
But see how deep the bullet lies"
— KATE BUSH, "RUNNING UP THAT HILL"

Miami, Florida—Sunday, December 19

"I got us a tree," Jamie announced on his way back from his and Eli's doughnut-and-coffee run the next morning. He triumphantly held up a small fake tree already decorated with lights; I could see the cord trailing out behind the thing.

"More importantly, I got coffee," Eli added, handing me a foam cup.

All of a sudden, it occurred to me to wonder where Jamie usually spent Christmas.

"Jamie," I said, sitting my coffee on the nightstand and running a hand through my bed-head hair. "Where are you going to go for Christmas?" I tried to sound gentle and not pushy, but from the look on his face, maybe it was a sore subject and I shouldn't have asked.

"I would usually go to see my mom," he said. "But I'm not going back there while she's married to that creep. So, nowhere. That's why I let some crazy girl kidnap me." He grinned, though it was a lopsided one that didn't quite reach the sadness in his eyes. "So are you gonna help me decorate this tree or what?"

"With what? Coffee stirrers and sugar packets?" Eli asked.

"O ye of little faith," I told him, getting up and going to my bag to grab the jewelry I knew was stuck in the front compartment. I sat cross-legged next to Jamie and the little tree and handed him a jumble of necklaces to untangle. "Here — some of these are kinda sparkly."

"Some." Jamie snorted, seeming glad for the distraction from his brief departure into serious land. "You like all that hippie stuff, Lexi. Everything you wear looks old. I don't mean ugly," he hurried to add. "Just antique-y."

"Most of it is," Eli told him. "Xa — Lexi never met a thrift store she didn't like."

"So what's it like in New York City this time of year?" Jamie asked. Eli started describing the tree at Rockefeller Center and all the lights. Jamie looked rapt.

"That's where we should have taken him," Eli observed. "You've never been to New York, have you?"

When Jamie shook his head, Eli then informed him that he hadn't yet truly lived.

I didn't say anything. I wasn't ready to go home. In fact, I didn't know if I ever would be.

I half expected Eli to suggest we jump in the car and head north, but he let the moment pass. Jamie and I decorated the tree, which now looked either very festive or a lot like a weird window display in a vintage shop, as Eli said.

"So when do we leave to find Nick?" Jamie asked as he plugged in the tree.

"I don't know where he lives," I admitted.

"That club of his cousin's, the one he basically owns — it's called Revenge," Jamie said. "A couple of us went down there last summer."

"How did you know I wanted to look for Nick?" I asked him.

Jamie snorted. "Have you met yourself?"

Eli didn't say anything, but he didn't meet my eyes, either.

"I don't have any clothes for a nightclub," I said. I looked down in dismay at my NINJAS HATE PIRATES T-shirt and holey denim skirt.

"Good thing Stan sent you a Hanukkah present." Eli held up a credit card and almost smiled.

"Hey, *I* need some new threads, too." Jamie vaulted over his tree, and I shoved my feet into my flip-flops and followed them out the door. This was shaping up to be the strangest Christmas ever.

After a trip to a very large mall, and a surprising amount of difficulty for me in finding a new top, the three of us hit the food court and then Jamie drove us back to the motel.

I kicked them out of the room for an hour so I could try

to look like a girl for a change. They left, chatting like old friends. Weird, weird, weird.

We got on the road a little after ten. Eli got directions for Revenge on his phone and guided Jamie, who was driving. Eli's car looked like a sad orphan in the part of downtown near the club. I felt the same about my clothes, my hair, my existence. But I'd come this far.

So there I was, standing in line to get into a club called Revenge, in Miami, where it was at least eighty-five degrees even though it was less than a week until Christmas. I stood beside my ex–best friend and the carnie guy I'd kissed once and then avoided. I played idly with my fake ID while I considered that this was *actually* my life.

"It's all-ages," Eli told me, looking toward the ID in my hands. Both Eli and I had fake IDs — we'd gotten them to see bands back in New York.

"Oh, that makes sense," I said, realizing Nick would hardly hang out in his own building and risk getting the place shut down. I looked at Eli as he stood beside me and had one of those nanoseconds of recalibration. I always thought of him as a younger version of himself, the one who existed before he'd started going to the gym — which had to be one of the signs of the apocalypse.

The line for Revenge was moderately long — by Manhattan standards, at least. Some loud guys walked toward us. I felt Eli grab my hand and step closer to me.

Of course this had the effect of making one of the guys

notice me, instead of the opposite. "Hey, mama." He stepped away from the pack and closer to me, looking me up and down. I felt Eli stiffen beside me. I wasn't really alarmed, just pondering how not-sexy it was to call someone who wasn't your mother *mama*. Jamie woke up and got in the guy's face. If you happen to feel compelled to go to a club in Miami to look for/stalk your crush, I'm telling you, two guys are better than one.

"She's with us," Jamie growled.

The guy grinned at me, apparently not up to no good. "'With us,' huh? You go, girl." He winked lasciviously at me.

"You have no idea," I told him, using a slightly lascivious voice myself.

He and the others walked off laughing, and Jamie turned around and gave me a surprised look. "You, Lexi Ryan, are not boring," he told me.

"I'm gonna take that as a compliment," I responded. Eli was still holding my hand, and I turned to him. His face was curiously distracted. I wondered what he was thinking about, but didn't ask because the line surged forward, and before I knew it we had made it past the bouncers and were walking into the club. Eli dropped my hand as we walked through the doorway.

The club was all black inside — black booths, black floor, exposed ducts and wiring in the ceiling that was painted — you guessed it — black. There were sconces with lights that looked like old-fashioned gaslights. A woman on the small stage was singing a slow song in a minor key. It was still early; I guessed the music would be more up-tempo later.

Jamie, Eli, and I looked at one another, not quite sure what to do or where to stand. This wasn't really any of our scenes, and I felt suddenly really stupid for dragging them here with me, for coming at all. And then I spotted Nick across the room.

He was surrounded by people, and a very tiny blond girl seemed to be doing her best to crawl into his pocket.

I couldn't breathe. Seeing him here, like this, was a punch to the stomach. He didn't seem like *my* Nick from the circus.

And then things got a whole lot worse.

We were standing close to the stage. I don't know how we got there; I think I was unconsciously walking toward Nick, even as he gave every evidence of not missing me or remembering my name. Jamie and Eli, bless them, had come along in my wake. I heard Eli clear his throat and say, "Um, X?" He elbowed me, a little too hard, making me think it hadn't been the first signal, and gestured toward the stage.

The woman up there was now singing an old Kate Bush song, "Running Up That Hill." The voice was familiar, because a long time ago, it used to sing me to sleep.

I stood there right in front of the stage and looked up at the very person I had come on this adventure to find.

I looked up to see the woman performing up there on stage was my mom.

CHAPTER TWENTY-FOUR

TURNS OUT I WAS STALKING MY MOTHER

"Another uninnocent, elegant fall into the unmagnificent lives of adults"

— THE NATIONAL, "MISTAKEN FOR STRANGERS"

The Nightmare That Is My Life — Sunday, December 19

"Um, that lady looks just like you." Jamie stood staring up at the stage, mouth open.

And she did. Callie Ryan, or whatever she was calling herself these days, looked almost exactly like me, except that she had hazel eyes that were almost gold. She had only been eighteen when she had me, and she looked very young up there. She was even dressed like me — in a black top and denim skirt — and her hair was wavy just like mine, and almost the same length. I felt sick.

Eli had grabbed my hand again, but I had the urge to take it back and wipe it on my skirt because it felt cold and sweaty, along with the rest of me.

I knew the exact moment she saw me standing there

because she stopped singing. Just awkwardly stopped — the band behind her kept playing. She stood there for a second, looking like someone had punched her, and then she ran backstage.

She was actually running away from me. My own mother was running away from me. I fought back tears. I mean, I hated her, but who should have this happen to them? Eli gripped my hand harder. Nick had noticed the snafu on stage, and then noticed us, had shaken off the blond and was walking toward us. I realized I wasn't so good with standing, but Nick was already behind me, and though Eli still had my hand, I realized I was leaning against Nick.

I heard his voice say my name, low in my ear, but whatever else he said I couldn't process.

And then my mother was standing in front of me; she seemed a little out of breath. There were tears coming out of her eyes, but she didn't make a sound until she said a few seconds later, "Lexi."

I was propped up by Nick and Eli, and I couldn't speak. I still hadn't been able to downshift from the impression that my mother was running away from me.

I saw Callie's eyes shift to Nick's; there was recognition there, and in her voice when she said his name a moment later. She sounded almost as confused as I felt.

Some kind of jarring techno music had been put on the sound system in place of the singer who now stood in front of me. It made my head hurt, but its discordant crashing noises seemed the perfect soundtrack for this moment. Some people had started dancing, and someone crashed into me, and I felt Nick steering me off what had now become the dance floor. I let him pull me along with him, and a minute later we had walked through the back of the club and into some kind of office. I heard Nick say something to Jamie, then he shut the door, and the crashing music grew instantly quieter.

I turned out of Nick's arms to him to ask for an explanation first, because I trusted him. I had trusted my mom, too, but that had been when I was eight.

"You know my mother." I didn't really phrase it as a question. "My mother works for you."

The room got a little bright for a second, and I felt unsure on my feet. Since Nick was all too familiar with my new, charming ability to faint, he took my unsteadiness as his cue to help me sit down on the black leather couch that took up most of the back wall of the office. I sat still for a second, closed my eyes, and reminded myself to breathe. When I opened them I saw that Eli was standing awkwardly by the door, clearly not wanting to leave me, but also not feeling comfortable about staying. Jamie, I was sure, had chosen the correct side of the closing door and was probably out making new friends in South Florida.

Nick was leaning against the desk that dominated the wall opposite the couch. My mother was standing between the two of us.

"So you were saying you know my mother." I wasn't letting Nick off the hook.

He nodded slowly. "Your mother has performed here before."

"And you knew who I was — I mean, who she was to me."

He nodded again. "I just figured it out. My cousin gave me some headshots and CDs to sort through, find some acts to book for the year. And when I saw her picture —"

"Nick called me," I heard Callie say. "And I'm so glad he did. Because I really need to talk to you, Lexi."

"What are you going to say to me, Mother?" I asked her. "Are you going to explain to me why you left me when I was a little kid and never checked on me? Are you going to explain why you took the money Gavin left for me and ran off with it?"

"Yes, Lexi — I'd like to explain all of those things. Especially the ones that aren't true." I felt the anger well up in me, and she saw it. "I'm a lot of things, Lexi, but I'm not a liar," she said fiercely. "I lied once, for what I thought was a good reason, but I learned my lesson. Please, just hear me out. Give me twenty minutes. I won't say you owe me that, but for your own sake, you should listen."

I nodded mutely. There had been something in her voice when she promised me she wasn't a liar, something that made me at least want to hear the rest.

I looked at Eli, standing by the door, and then at Nick. As nice as it had been to lean on both of them, I suddenly wanted them to not hear whatever Callie had to say. Or see my reaction to whatever it was. Eli figured it out first. "Um,

Nick, maybe we should give them some privacy. We'll be right outside."

I nodded and watched them leave the office. I got up off the couch and started pacing. Callie took the place that Nick had abandoned and leaned against the desk. I heard her draw a deep breath, but I couldn't bring myself to look at her.

"First, I am so sorry about your father. I am so, so sorry. You were . . . alone. Because I was gone." Callie's voice sounded angry, and I thought she was probably angry at herself until she said, "But for purely selfish reasons, I have to say I'm glad he's gone."

My head jerked up at that. "What?"

She raked hands through her hair in frustration. "I don't want to speak badly about Gavin to you, Lexi. It's not right. But I can't explain this to you any other way. I don't want to make your life any harder than it's already been. But you need to understand what happened. Why I left."

"I don't think you could make it any harder than you already have. And you left because you wanted to leave," I said, each word deliberate. "It's the only explanation — otherwise, why no contact? No nothing for the past decade . . ."

I looked at her briefly and saw that she wiped a tear out of the corner of her eye. Then I looked away again. I didn't want to feel sorry for her.

"I didn't leave, Lexi. Not exactly. I was forced out."

"You were forced out of where, the city? Um, sorry, I

don't remember exactly everything about the world from the time I was eight, but I'm pretty sure it was a free country then, too."

"It was Gavin."

"Why would Dad do that? *How* would he do that?"

She hesitated, pushing herself away from the side of the desk, and then she started to pace. I sat back down on the edge of the couch. "I did something, something very wrong. I had an affair. Gavin found out about it. That's the lie I mentioned. It was with one of our friends. There is . . . no excuse for that, what I did. I'm not going to try to make excuses. Gavin and I had problems, we had grown apart, I thought I loved Max . . . but in the end, all of those things are just excuses. I broke my marriage vows, and Gavin was . . . well, at first he was hurt. But then it turned into something else."

"He was really mad at you," I supplied in a small voice, remembering. Callie was right. It started out with a broken heart. And then Gavin had been really angry. All that anger had been meant for the woman pacing in front of me, but since she had been gone, it had landed lots of other places instead. Like on me.

"There was this one time I forgot to feed Mrs. Henderson's cat," I began. Mrs. Henderson had lived next door to us for my whole life. Every fall she went back home to Pennsylvania for a week, and we took care of Oscar, her cat — a series of cats named Oscar, really. "I forgot to feed Oscar number three when I was supposed to. Gavin turned over the dining room table, and all that stuff was still on top of it, and it all broke, went everywhere . . ."

I couldn't bring myself to keep telling this story, though. Gavin hadn't hurt me, just scared me. He had gotten so much more chill over the years, I'd made myself forget that time. I looked at Callie and saw that her face had drained of color.

"I'm so sorry, Lexi. I know it's not enough, but I am. That anger that you saw, there was a time when I got the full force of it. I did betray him, but what he did to me . . ." Her voice had begun to quaver, but she took a deep breath, closed her eyes, and then spoke in a low voice she kept even, almost monotone. She had stopped pacing and stood motionless in the center of the little office. "Your father hired a service to pack up everything that was mine; it was all sitting in the lobby of the building, labeled with my first name and my maiden name. He closed our joint account, served me with divorce papers. He was very . . . efficient in the way he got rid of me."

"Okay, so Dad kicked you out and all that. I know you guys went to court. But that doesn't explain why you didn't take me. Or at least ask for partial custody. Or even visitation. I never saw you again, not until today."

Her eyes closed again, and she took a deep breath. "I did ask." She sighed. "I did," she repeated fiercely.

"But why? You were my mother — I thought they usually ruled for the mom in custody cases."

"I guess they do, when the mom isn't so messed up." Her

voice was louder now. "I tried — I asked for full custody. But I was twenty-six years old, had cheated on my husband. I sat down in court that first day and faced that same man, the one I thought I'd loved, and he was sitting on *Gavin's* side of the table. Gavin convinced him — probably paid him — to testify against me. And I'd never held a decent job, had no money. Gavin's family had so much money, and those lawyers. When they were done painting their picture of me, I sounded much worse than I was. They dragged out some charges from when I was nineteen. They even convinced the judge that I'd been abusive to you."

"But you weren't!" Whatever Callie had done before or after, she hadn't been that sort of mom. As much as it killed me to admit it, even to myself, she'd been a good mother, for the brief time I'd had her.

Her voice dropped to the smallest whisper. "But I was — once. It was a very bad day, I was so angry that day, and you weren't listening to me. You wanted your father, you kept saying, 'I want to play with Daddy!' But he was at work, like always. You just kept asking for him, and I needed to go out to the store, but you wouldn't budge. I picked you up and . . . I shook you . . . pretty hard — I mean, I shouldn't have shaken you at all. Gavin came home, caught me — he stopped me. It was when you were very small, maybe three . . . and it never happened again."

Callie took another ragged breath and looked up at me. "From that time on, Gavin got in my head. I had already told him about how my father was with me. And he had me half-convinced that I was set to go down the same path. He kept asking me about what I did all day, and I'd tell him, and then he would ask again, like he was trying to trip me up." Callie broke off and started crying. She lowered her head right where she stood and let the tears run down her face. I sat frozen for a long minute.

Finally after what seemed like forever, she sighed before continuing. "I lost custody. I was only offered court-supervised visitation of my own child — of you. I should have taken it — I know — I *know* that, now." Her voice broke. "But back then, I felt so small, so horrible, and like I was so bad for you. In the end I convinced myself that you would be better off without me. So I left, and I didn't go back."

The planet tilted on its axis; I felt it shift beneath me. The colors, even in the dark office, seemed too vivid, like I was in a painting. Everything I thought I knew about the last eight — or more — years. It was all different. Maybe even wrong.

"Why did he do all that?" I finally breathed.

"Gavin thought he was doing what was best for you," Callie said. There was a folding chair beside the couch, and she picked it up, set it up, and then sat down, concentrating like it was a very complicated task. She then went on to speak even more carefully. "He was a good father to you. He didn't expect to be dead at forty-one. If he hadn't been killed, you would have been fine, as you were before. But that's why I said from a selfish point of view, I'm glad. If he hadn't died, you never would have come to find me."

"But why . . ." I was still putting the pieces together as I spoke aloud. "Why did Dad's lawyer tell me that he left me money, and that he'd sent it to you?"

Callie's face filled suddenly with such hatred, much more extreme than what had shown on her face when she'd talked about Dad. "Is this lawyer of your dad's named Max Neville?"

"Oh my God!" I yelled. "*That* Max — the guy you . . ." I trailed off, not sure how to phrase it.

"If there was any money, Max probably kept it," she said scornfully. "But what I'm trying to figure out is, how did you get to the Europa show?"

"Max Neville," I told her. "He said he tracked you down."

I watched a series of emotions play across my mom's face: anger, pain, and something else, something soft, just for a moment — a yearning that she soon mastered. Max had completely betrayed her, but she had loved him. And maybe he had tried in some small way to make up for what he had done to her. He'd sent me to her. At least, he would have, if she had still been at Europa when I'd arrived. As it was, it took Nick to bring us together.

"So Nick called you — is that how you got here?"

"It was his cousin Dominic who called and hired me, offered a great rate, said he really wanted to get me back down here. Now I guess I know why he was so adamant about it — or at least why Nick was. I think he wanted it to be a surprise." She rolled her eyes and made a rueful face. "Surprise."

"Understatement," I managed. I shook my head. "I just can't get over it, about Dad."

"He loved you more than anything, and he wanted to keep you with him. And he couldn't bear for me to be in his sight. So in a way, he did what he had to do. I played my part in it, too, Lexi. I admit it. And I hate that I had to tear him down in your eyes for you to even think about giving me a chance. But he's . . . he's gone, and I think whatever I may have owed him is paid. I want a chance with you now, if you think you can give me that."

"I don't know," I told her. "This is a lot to take in. This is a continent to take in. And I got pretty used to hating you."

She nodded. Her eyes were wet, but she didn't cry again. I nodded back.

We walked together toward the door that led back into the club, to the rest of the world. And the rest of my life, maybe with my mother back in it.

CHAPTER TWENTY-FIVE

I HATE CELL PHONES

"I think I need a sunrise
I'm tired of the sunset"
— AUGUSTANA, "BOSTON"

Miami, Florida — The Second-Longest Night of My Life

Callie went to apologize to the band and to Nick's cousin. I had faith in her. If she could get me to even consider forgiving her, those guys should be cake.

Nick was back to work when we returned, as in working the room, which seemed to be his unofficial job. He was sort of wearing a black-haired stick figure clad in tall boots with high heels. I felt so young, so awkward, and I resented him for making me feel that way.

When he spotted me, he untangled his limbs from the stick and made his way to me. I saw that Eli had been sitting over in the corner, and he started walking toward me, too, but Nick got there first.

"Are you all right?"

I had no idea how to answer that question. "I'm . . . I'm . . . I don't know. She told me lots of things. She thought you maybe wanted to surprise me — when you figured out who she was? Is that why you didn't call me?"

The rational part of my brain knew that I hadn't called him, either, but that part of my brain wasn't really functional just then. I had been waiting for him to call me — and he hadn't, not for a solid week. I could take a hint. Of course, then I disregarded that hint and came chasing after him like a crazy person, but that was beside the point.

"Callie's right, it was meant to be a surprise — for Christmas. I was hoping to bring her to you — to where I *thought* you were — later this week."

"No, I mean, why haven't you called me? At *all* . . ."

"I've called you — a few times. You didn't answer. It just rings and rings."

I pulled out the crummy pay-as-you-go phone that it turned out my mom's ex-boyfriend had bought me. It lit up, but the screen was blank. "Are you kidding me?" I cried. I threw the phone against the wall at the back of the club.

"Remind me never to get you a decent phone," Nick said, leading me back into the little office.

"I had a nice phone once," I heard myself say softly when we got inside. Eli had been watching me with Nick, but he hadn't come any closer.

Nick wrapped his arms around me, though there was something different in this embrace, different from before. He held me a little apart from him. And suddenly, I knew. I understood it all. I stepped back out of the circle of his arms.

"You found my mother and you were bringing her to me," I told him.

"Yes," he said, sounding wary of the tone of my voice.

"You found my mother and you were bringing her to me," I repeated. "You didn't want me to be alone, or in trouble. So you could leave me and not feel bad." I saw the truth of my words in his eyes. "Why?" I managed, though the word barely disturbed the air.

He shook his head sadly and reached out for me, but I stepped back. "Lexi, you know why. We're not in the same place. You need to go to college."

"I'll go to college!" I told him. "It's not like prison. They let you out to, like, see people — all the time."

"Lexi, this isn't going to work. You and I both know it."

"You have a girlfriend here," I said, remembering the blond and the stick. "Or girlfriends."

He shook his head. "Lexi, I don't have a girlfriend, or I would never have . . . back at Europa . . . But the fact remains, I still should not have let you — let myself. But I'm stopping it. Now."

"You don't want to see me?" I asked, not looking at him, looking at some promotional poster in the office like it was the most interesting thing in the entire stupid world. I knew that if I looked at him I would start crying.

"No, Lexi," I heard him say, and his voice sounded sure. "I don't want us to see each other anymore."

I nodded, eyes still on the poster. "I understand," I heard

myself say. "Good-bye, then, Nick. Thanks for finding my mom."

I turned around to leave, but he didn't let me. He pulled me back against him and hugged me, hard. So then I did cry. I leaned back, far enough to look in his eyes. I saw the resolve there and knew I wasn't going to change his mind. I pulled away, opened the door, and walked out of the office, and then straight toward the door of the club. I felt Eli's hand grab mine and saw Jamie out of the corner of my eye. They walked with me out of Nick's club and into the night. Callie was already standing on the sidewalk, a small suitcase beside her.

"Are you ready to go home?" Jamie asked me.

I didn't know whether *home* was the motel room with the seagulls or my room in Lina's trailer back in Frostproof, but either way, I was ready. I nodded and let my weird little family take me away from the street in Miami where my heart had been broken twice in one night.

CHAPTER TWENTY-SIX

HOLES

"And please remember me, seldomly
In the car behind the carnival
. . . you turn from me
And said the trapeze act was wonderful
But never meant to last"
— IRON & WINE, "THE TRAPEZE SWINGER"

Frostproof, Florida — Monday, December 20

I knocked on Lina's trailer door since I had a long-lost mother in tow. But she didn't hear, so I let myself in. She and Liska were watching *Elf* — Lina lying on the couch and Liska on the floor.

"So, I went to Miami," I announced.

"Yeah, got your note," Lina said, not looking up.

"And I sort of found my mom." That got their attention. "Lina and Liska, this is my mother."

"Hi," Callie said, giving a little wave.

Liska scrambled to her feet, and Lina sat up. I saw Liska locate the remote and hit the mute button. "It's nice to meet you," the sisters said almost in unison.

"Um, Lex? How *did* you get to Miami?" Lina asked. "And, uh, why was your mom there?"

"It's a long story," I told her. "Callie is going to stay for a . . . bit. If that's okay. Can you think of a place . . . ?"

"She can sleep here," Lina said. "I can sleep at Liska's."

"No, I don't want —" I began.

"I don't want to put you out," Callie said at the same time.

"No worries." Lina flopped back down on the couch and unmuted the TV. "Why don't you show your mom around?" She laughed then at Will Ferrell attacking the department store Santa, and I led Callie out of the trailer. In the off-season, these energetic circus people were seriously dedicated to the pursuit of the couch-and-remote lifestyle.

I was showing Callie the ring when we ran into Louie.

"You!" he said to her. "I know you. From the show people, right?"

Callie nodded. "Yes, Mr. Vrana. It's good to see you again."

I guess Louie *had* remembered a Callie, after all.

"Louie, please! It's a shame that all didn't work out," he said, shaking his head. Then he seemed to notice me. "I should have remembered — you look so much alike. But you found her anyway. Good for you, Lexi! Such a clever girl, your daughter!"

"I really didn't do anything," I mumbled. I mean, I had driven to Miami, but I hadn't been looking for Callie.

"Will you be here for the holiday, Mrs. . . . ?"

"Just call me Callie. And, yes, I'd like to stay, if it's okay with you."

"Of course! The more the merrier," Louie said. "We will see you later!" He clapped Callie on the back, patted my head, and continued on his way.

I turned to Callie. "The show people? So you *were* here?"

Callie nodded. "For about a week. I was hired to perform in the show — Louie had hired a new director, and he was going to expand that part — I was going to sing and act in the skits. But the first week I was here, Louie and the guy he'd hired had a huge fight, and the guy walked off. And that was the end of that."

"Well, not entirely," I said archly. "I mean, here we are."

"Good point." Callie laughed.

On Christmas Eve day, Jamie managed to get Lina and Liska unglued from the couch, and the three of them brought Eli and me along on a Walmart run. We found another little tree, and Jamie found strings of one hundred lights for a dollar ninety-nine; he could not be restrained. When we got back he started stringing them everywhere. Lina and Liska brought Callie and me with them to help Louie with the cooking; we helped him make a giant turkey, about five kinds of potatoes, and then sugar cookies.

When I came out of Louie's trailer, pleasantly tired and smelling of food, I saw that Jamie had rigged up the swings. I'd once told him they were my favorite ride. Jamie was blasting weird indie rock from my iPod out of one of the big Hurricane speakers. Louie didn't even say anything about the power Jamie was using as he rigged up the big generators.

I sat in the basket seat and watched the trees and Louie's and Lina's trailers swing around and around until the landscape was a blur. It was great up here, because the tears didn't even have a chance to fall down my face; the wind just carried them away.

The speakers were playing Iron & Wine's "The Trapeze Swinger." Jamie had scrolled through my songs and picked it — probably for Lina. It was a sad song, and it made me cry even when I wasn't a heartbroken mess on Christmas. I listened to the words on the super-powered speaker that was designed to be heard over the much-louder Hurricane and a ride full of screaming teenagers: "But please remember me, my misery, and how it lost me all I wanted," Sam sang, and I cried for what I had never known about my parents, and what I hadn't even known I'd lost. And I cried for losing and finding Eli again, and for what I had dared to hope for with Nick.

Jamie stopped the ride as the song ended, and I put my feet on the ground. He took one look at my face and said to Eli, "Well, that was an awesome idea."

We ate outside at the big folding table. Tonight for our Christmas Eve feast, there was lots of extra space, though Louie and his daughters had pretty much covered every inch of the table's surface with bowls and platters of food. I didn't notice that the silent Eddie had reappeared until I looked down the table and saw him going to town on a turkey leg.

The night was warm and clear, and the Walmart twinkle lights added a festive air to the party. My Christmas playlist was playing. I sat between Callie and Eli. Lina and Louie were teasing Liska, and their laughter was infectious. I smiled at Callie when she turned to pass me the third kind of potatoes. I didn't feel normal around her yet. But losing Gavin had led, in a strange and complicated way, to getting her back. It was sort of a Christmas miracle.

I didn't let myself think too much about what she had told me about my dad. It was exhausting, all this compartmentalizing and managing of my brain. I felt like I could sleep for a week. And all these potatoes and the tryptophan in the turkey were probably not going to help. Then again, sleeping for a week sounded kind of nice. And I was, for the moment, on hiatus.

I heard Jamie's distinctive laugh and looked up to see him majorly flirting with Lina. I had called *that* a long time ago.

When most of us were done eating (except Eddie), Jamie stood up and pulled Lina along with him, spinning her around expertly. My mix had landed on "Winter Wonderland" by the Cocteau Twins, and the sweet and ethereal song was perfect for the graceful couple Jamie and Lina made. I laughed as I watched Louie drag his other daughter to her feet, and they joined in, though they made a less well-matched and graceful pair.

Eli stood beside me. "Dance with me, Lexi?" I heard him ask, his voice low.

I turned around to look at him: my best friend. I had really believed I'd lost him forever, that he would remain a sore spot I would have to avoid for the rest of my life. But he had come here to find me, had missed Hanukkah with his own family, and was now here in this field celebrating Christmas with what was left of mine. I took his hand and let him lead me to where the others were dancing.

The song changed, and "Fairytale of New York" by The Pogues came on. Eli took me carefully in his arms, and I heard him say under his breath, "Perfect." It's a sweet-sounding song that takes a dark turn.

We didn't dance like we were contestants on *Dancing with the Stars*, like Jamie and Lina, nor as exuberantly as Louie and Liska. It felt strange to raise my arms up to rest on Eli's shoulders. We hadn't been that close together since that night. The memory of that night was so intertwined with what had happened later, it was no wonder I had stayed away from him.

"I wasn't sure you'd say yes," Eli said, his voice still low in my ear. "Of course, I wasn't sure you were ever going to talk to me again," he said, his tone light, though I sensed the tension beneath his words. "It was touch and go there for a while."

"But you stayed," I told him. He nodded, but did not speak. Instead, in response he pulled me closer against him, his hands tightening on my waist. I was wearing my little black cotton dress in honor of the occasion, and I had even used Lina's curling iron to add ringlets to my hair. I thought at the time I'd been trying to get in the holiday spirit by looking pretty for a change. Now I was afraid that wasn't the only reason. Either some stupid corner of my heart still hoped that Nick would pull one of his sudden appearing acts, or I'd been thinking of Eli. Or worse: both.

Eli pulled me even tighter to him, putting his hand behind my neck and gently resting my head against his chest. I felt my pulse start to race faster. What was the matter with me? Why did Eli still have this effect on me?

I pulled my head from his shoulder, but gently, not breaking away from him, or the spell of the dance, completely. "You broke my heart, you know," I told him.

He nodded, his jaw tense, his eyes dark on mine. "I broke mine, too, that morning. And then you were gone, and I couldn't even tell you . . ." His voice trailed off. I realized all of a sudden that we weren't dancing anymore, just standing close together, arms around each other. I looked around quickly and saw that everyone else had vanished, back into Louie's trailer. Jamie had even turned the volume on the music down low.

"Will you ever be able to really forgive me?" he asked me.

"I don't know," I answered. "It's more complicated than that. You left me before I ran out that morning."

He sighed. "I know," he said. "At the time, I was stupid. I wanted both of you." His voice had dropped so low, I almost couldn't hear him.

"I can't imagine what that's like," I said dryly, deliberately lightening the mood a little, and at the same time reminding him that since he'd been out of the picture there had been someone else for me, too.

"We can't stay here forever," he said.

"I know," I told him. "But New York isn't home in the way it used to be. Things won't ever be the same again — for me, at least."

"But the city's still your home," he pressed. "You can still go to college, like you planned. Callie will help you — and I'll help you."

I nodded, feeling hollow. There were two holes in my chest now. The one I had been carrying around since Gavin died seemed to have expanded. And then there was the one Nick Tarus had made.

"I don't know what I want to do," I heard myself tell Eli. "I don't know anything anymore."

Eli drew me close again for a hug. I guess he looked at his watch, too, because he told me, "Hey — it's midnight." I looked up at him, and he whispered, "Merry Christmas, Lexi." And we started dancing again.

CHAPTER TWENTY-SEVEN

"Happy New Year" Is a Really Annoying Phrase, Actually

*"And I feel nothing, not brave
It's a hard day for breathing again"*
— Rilo Kiley, "Paint's Peeling"

Frostproof, Florida — Saturday, January 1

I knew I couldn't hide out with Louie, Lina, and Liska forever, not now that my mom was back in the picture. I had a prepaid semester of Sheldon to claim, now that I had a legal guardian in tow. And after that, college.

Knowing I had to leave didn't make it any easier. Lina had tears in her eyes, though she didn't let go of Jamie's hand as she hugged me good-bye outside Eli's car.

"I will miss you, my second sister," she told me. "You will always have a home here if you want one."

Then she made fun of *me* for crying; but her words had touched a nerve. A home: That's what she and Louie and Liska had given me, when I didn't have one and needed one so desperately. I sniffed hard, trying to get control of my tears.

"This isn't good-bye," I told her. "Louie promised I could have my job back this summer," I reminded her. *College* wasn't prepaid, and Callie didn't have a steady job yet, so I knew I would need a summer job, and being able to come back at the end of the semester seemed like the perfect solution.

Jamie presented me with the Miami tree as we were leaving. I accepted it happily, especially since it was still decorated with most of my jewelry. "Be good in the big bad city," he told me.

Liska hugged me and told me to be careful, too, and that she looked forward to seeing me in the summer. When she pulled away from me, her eyes were wet, but Lina didn't tease her, wisely. Lina and I exchanged a look over Liska's head, and Lina said, "I told you so," about her sister who I had once thought was so cold.

In the car, I sat in the backseat with Callie. It was a little awkward at first, but then we all started eating snacks and drinking sodas, and I felt myself loosen up, remembering how it used to feel to be with her. She seemed so familiar — and she looked so much like me, it was hard to feel awkward for long around her. Callie hadn't brought up Gavin again, which under the circumstances suited me just fine. Eli was quiet, for Eli, in the front, but was acting silly along with us by the time we pulled into the huge airport parking lot.

"Why are we flying again when we have a car?" I asked as Eli parked.

"Because my aunt lives in Orlando, and I'm selling her the car," he told me. "My uncle's gonna drive her here to pick it up. And because class starts the day after tomorrow." He caught my eyes in the rearview mirror. "You do remember school?"

"Vaguely," I said with asperity. "I can't see what the rush is; I've already missed, um, the entire year."

"Exactly," he told me. "If you have any hope of graduating, you have to be there for all of second semester. As it is you'll be doubling up with the courses you missed first term."

"Ugh." I sat back against the seat. "What about you?" I challenged. "You missed some, too."

"I was there for most of it," he told me. "I think I can go back and take the finals and be okay."

"You suck," I told him as Callie and I climbed out of the backseat.

"I know," he smiled, grabbing my worldly goods and hoisting them on his back as he shut the trunk.

Eli bought me a mocha from Starbucks and sat down beside me in the chairs at the gate. "Where's Callie?" he asked.

"Calling somebody," I said. "She's trying to figure out where we're going to live. She hasn't said anything, but I don't think that she's exactly New York real estate flush."

"I know, that's why I gave up the car," Eli said. I looked at him in surprise. "I mean, who can afford a car in New

York?" he asked, and I realized I had misunderstood. For a minute there, I'd been worried that he meant he planned to give us the money toward our housing dilemma. "I'd say you could stay with us," he went on, "but I'm not too sure I'm even going to be allowed back home. And under the circumstances —"

"I get it," I stopped him, pulling the lid off my mocha and taking my first sip.

"Why do you always pull the lid off?" Eli asked.

"I like the foam," I told him. "So, Callie and I are going to live in maybe, like, Brooklyn," I warned him. "I'd say that's best-case scenario."

"And Jersey City is worst-case?"

"Hope not." I laughed. "We are such snobs."

"Yeah," he said. "But it's our birthright. But don't worry — I'll take the train, or the PATH train, whatever. We'll still see each other." He looked at me. "That is, if you want to see me."

I met his eyes. "I want to," I told him. It was getting easier to see him and not think of all the bad stuff. And right then, I thought of something — of someone — I had managed almost, to my shame, to forget.

"Oh my God — Bailey!" I sat up, splashing a little mocha on myself.

"I told you not to take the lid off," Eli said, his face unreadable.

I ignored that comment. "Eli, we can't hang out together at school. It's too mean. We've already been awful enough —"

"Lex, it's okay," he said. "Bailey transferred to Sidwell."

I slumped in my seat, more relieved than I had a right to be. "I shouldn't feel happy about that. I'm a horrible person."

"No, you're not."

"I'm pretty sure I am. But I'm also pretty sure I can't ever make this up to her. And that maybe if I apologized it would just bring it all back for her. I think the nicest thing I can do for her now is never see her again. Is that being selfish?"

"Wouldn't you feel better if you could apologize to her?"

I thought about that. "Maybe. But I still don't think it's right — not now."

"Then you're being the opposite of selfish. It's going to be hard enough for you to go back there, I know. You sort of need one thing, at least, to be easier. And I know for a fact that she's happier never seeing *my* face again, so it all works out."

"Yeah, it all works out," I said, my voice a little flat, as I watched Callie walking toward us. If only it didn't all work out so that *everybody's* heart got broken.

"Happy New Year!" The perky flight attendant smiled at me as I shuffled off the plane. One of the flight crew — maybe the captain, maybe not, but he looked a little like a Ken doll come to life — added his own "Happy New Year" in a husky voice. I didn't take it personally. He had flirted with every other passenger — he was clearly one of those people who flirted as often as they breathed.

For some reason, this whole New Year's thing was really bothering me. I guess because I had just landed in my home state, so instead of new, today I was going back to old. And I had messed things up so badly in the old place, and, apparently, so had my dad, that I wasn't really sure how much I wanted to go there. My room, my home, weren't there anymore, and I was facing an uncertain future with a rather flaky mom.

Happy New Year.

When we left the airport, Callie gave the cab driver an address near our old neighborhood. "I found us a sublet," she said, smiling tentatively at me.

It was a sunny two-bedroom walk-up, fully furnished but uncluttered. After we got our bags inside, Callie and I walked to the diner she always used to take me to.

"You nervous about school Monday?" she asked me as we ate.

Somewhere in the diner, "Scar Tissue" by the Red Hot Chili Peppers was playing. Seemed appropriate for the moment. I felt like I had so many barely healed emotional bruises, the thought of going back to school was almost not something I could reconcile myself to doing. "Yeah," I heard myself say.

"High school sucks," Callie said, grabbing a fry from my plate and smiling. She was always doing that, alternating typical mom-type stuff, like, *Are you nervous about school Monday?* with comments like *High school sucks*, which made her seem more like my friend. Of course, Dad had been like that, too. They really were — had been — a lot alike. I wondered what went wrong. I both desperately wanted to know and not to know.

"At least Eli will be there," she told me. "He'll help you get reacclimated."

"I guess," I said. I didn't add that seeing Eli was still almost more stressful than school. I had not told her about the night Dad died — she seemed to have guessed the most important part, but I knew I was going to my grave without ever telling the story of the morning after to anyone. It was bad enough Eli existed in the world to know it, too.

"We have to get up early tomorrow," she observed, frowning a little. "We were lazy last week at Europa."

"Yep," I said, listlessly making a French-fry pyramid.

"I've never seen you not eat fries," Callie told me.

I didn't point out how many fry-eating opportunities of mine she had, in fact, missed. Things were still too tenuous. "I'm okay."

"I'm sorry everything's so hard right now."

"It's not your fault." She shot me a look. "Okay, it's nowhere near *all* your fault," I amended, making myself smile at her.

"Thanks for that," she said. "Oh, hey, wait — I got you something. It's not an amazing phone, but I took in the old one and got you the same number."

I couldn't help but smile as I accepted the small silver

phone. Maybe this one would actually last the year. "Thanks, Callie. That's really nice of you."

"It's nothing. I just want to thank you for — you know — letting me keep you, or at least trying it out until college. I mean it, Lexi. You'll never know how grateful I am."

I nodded, tears unaccountably pricking my eyes. "'S okay," I mumbled.

I poked at the half burger lying on my plate, thinking about Eli. He'd wanted to join us for dinner, but I had talked him out of it. I knew he would be busy making amends with his own parents for running away, spending his college money on a car, and missing school since early December.

So it was just Callie and me. It was both comforting and surreal to be back in my old neighborhood. Absolutely everything had changed for me, but looking around, everything here looked exactly the same.

CHAPTER TWENTY-EIGHT

MAYBE NOT INVISIBLE, BUT DEFINITELY OBLIVIOUS

"Never get noticed
Never get judged"
— RADIOHEAD, "LITTLE BY LITTLE"

13 Broome Street — Wednesday, January 5

"I heard she went crazy and stole a car. They had to legit lock her up. In *Florida*. Can you even imagine?"

This comment was the best one. I wish I hadn't been in a bathroom stall, unable to find out who said it, so I could have asked them to write it in my yearbook.

The rumors were flying about me and Eli. I was definitely no longer invisible, and it made me weirdly happy. It was sort of a thrill to hear people actually talking about me. (It wouldn't last, of course; I was pretty sure I'd be back to being part of the walls by graduation.) The fact that Bailey had left soon after I did only added fuel to the fire.

I was thinking a lot about Bailey lately, now that I was

back in these hallways and classrooms, where she and I had once been friends. Bailey may not have always been a perfect friend, might have taken advantage of me sometimes — but I had let her. If I hadn't learned anything else in the last four months, it was that I didn't want to be Doormat Girl ever again. I just hoped she was happy at her new school. Just hoped she'd be happy again, period.

First thing Monday, I had an appointment with the headmaster. As I walked toward the office, my stomach felt like I had a dead ferret in there. I'd heard from Eli that there was a new headmaster, though, which made me happy. Dr. Cranston had never exactly been crazy about me. Her compassion for me at the worst moment of my life would have fit in one of those little triangular paper cups she kept in her office by the water cooler.

This new headmaster had to see me differently, though; I had to make sure that he did. I'd made a New Year's resolution, one I was determined to keep: I was going to take school seriously. I was going to go in there and murder this last semester, and apply and get into a great college. Somehow.

The headmaster's name was Dr. Browning. I sat carefully in one of the chairs that faced his big desk.

"Miss Ryan," he intoned, disapproval evident in his voice. "You've had quite a year," he observed, laying what I assumed was my student file down on his desk.

Browning had embraced the stereotype and was wearing actual tweed, complete with those weird little elbow patches on his jacket. Those have always bothered me — what were they for? Just in case a sudden game of rugby erupted and he didn't have time to shuck his jacket? I pulled my attention back to the meeting at hand and reminded myself of my resolution.

"I really have," I told him.

"I'm very sorry about your father," he said next, surprising me. "And I must apologize, it seems, for my predecessor's handling of your . . . situation. She ought to have assisted you in locating your mother. I hold Eleanor Cranston largely responsible for your having to hare off to parts unknown to track down your parent." He actually sounded sort of angry. I enjoyed his use of *hare* as a verb and felt myself relax a little.

"But," he went on, "as Dr. Cranston is now the problem of the Immaculate Heart School in Boston, we shall move on. Thankfully, it seems, in looking at your records, that you will be able to complete your senior year this semester, with sufficient credits for graduation. I imagine that is your wish?"

I nodded. "Yes, sir. I absolutely want to graduate. I'll take whatever classes I need to."

"You missed an English credit and world history last term," he told me, "and this semester you need to take physics to complete the science requirement. Many of the other seniors will have a far less taxing schedule," he warned. "But you can do it if you set your mind to it."

"I can — I will."

"Very well," he said. "I will see to it your schedule is changed. Miss Ryan." He leaned forward then, almost smiled. He seemed like a serious guy, even though he was probably not that much older than my mom. But his eyes were a nice, kind brown. Of course, he would have been an improvement on Cranston had he been an actual snake.

"Miss Ryan, I think it is very admirable how you have managed your circumstances these last few months. You found yourself in very dire straits, and you seem to have kept your wits about you, all on your own, and come out just fine. Though I hadn't met you until today, only read your file, I am proud of you. You may find, having come through the crucible of such an experience, that you will now have a clearer sense of who you are and what you want. I hope that you will use this knowledge wisely."

He stood then and I belatedly followed suit; he shook my hand and sent me on my way.

I was back, easy as that. Thanks to Nick Tarus, who found my mother; Eli Katz, who gave up his college money to buy a car and come get me; and Callie, for coming back to New York with me and being my parent again. And I owed massive thanks to Lina and her father and her sister for taking me in, feeding me, and giving me a job. Dr. Browning had been wrong about that one thing: I hadn't done it all on my own, in the end.

I threw myself into schoolwork; I had enough catch-up work to keep me busy every night. I got into a routine in the new little apartment. It didn't really feel like ours — Callie had sublet the place from a friend, and her decor was still in place. I didn't even hang up my gargoyle lights in the tiny second bedroom. Callie had tried to give me the biggest one, one of the many manifestations of her guilt, but I didn't want to let her guilt turn me into an evil princess, so I turned her down. Compared to the room I'd had in Lina's trailer, my new digs were gigantic. There was a bed with a pretty light yellow quilt, and matching curtains. At first I put the ring Nick had given me on the top of the dresser, but then I decided to put it in a drawer.

Lina and I Skyped sometimes, but it was hard, because when she wasn't working, I was in school. She kept me updated on all the Europa gossip. The first time we spoke, the show was outside Baltimore, and I wished I had a car so I could just go see everyone in person. Not that missing any more school was actually an option.

Eli would walk me home every afternoon, but then he had to go straight home. He was a step beyond grounded for running off to Florida — something closer to house arrest: school, work at his uncle's deli (to pay back the college fund), homework, and bed. But he never complained, not to me, anyway.

As for Callie, she was a little bit like a caged bird. Before she got a job, she was always dutifully on her perch when I came home from school. But it only took her two weeks to find a pretty decent job as a receptionist in a dentist's office nearby. I could see the marks of strain, though. *She* was the real gypsy — though not a fortune teller, clearly, given her life choices. But I was grateful to her for going through the motions of boring-ness for me, for staying put when she wanted to roam.

As part of my get-into-college resolution, I rejoined the yearbook staff. I had joined for much the same reason at the beginning of the year, and had started going to meetings, but of course I'd missed most of the work putting the book together.

One afternoon, when I was typing in names for the colophon, I was surprised to see my name listed in with the rest of the staff. I told the assistant editor, Samantha, "You didn't need to put me in there."

She looked up from the computer screen across from me. "What are you doing right now?" she asked me.

"I'm typing in names," I said, puzzled.

Samantha sighed. "I mean, are you working on the yearbook?" she asked.

"Um, is that a trick question?"

"You wouldn't think so." She snorted. "You're working on the yearbook. Therefore, you are on the yearbook staff, genius." She smiled, taking all the sting out of the insult.

I looked at her and realized in that second that I had never really noticed Samantha Myers before — if I had, I would have seen someone who could have, maybe, been my friend at Sheldon. If I hadn't been walking around with my mind made up about everyone in this place.

"You know, I've been meaning to tell you, I was actually a little mad at you while you were gone," Samantha said.

"Why?"

"We voted for senior superlatives right before you left, do you remember?"

"Yeah, I think so."

"You got one — did you know?"

"Most likely to be invisible?" I asked. I wasn't the most anything else in this class. Or hadn't been, until I'd gained a smidge of notoriety from my disappearing act.

Samantha laughed. "No, you got most likely to never leave New York." She raised her eyebrows at me. "I got a really good candid of you and Eli out on the steps, looking very permanently rooted here, I might add. I designed the spread, and then boom — you took off and proved us all wrong! I had to redo the whole spread and use Tish Morgan and James Andrews instead."

"Me and Eli?" I asked.

"Yeah, he was voted the guy most likely never to leave," she said, laughing, "and then *he* left, too!"

"That's funny," I told her. "Me and Eli getting voted for that."

"It's not all that surprising," Samantha said. "We all knew you were both going to college here, probably getting married to each other, and having hipster babies."

"Getting married? Me and Eli?" I was horrified to realize my voice had just come out really high-pitched.

"Well, lots of people thought that," Samantha said, sounding a tad defensive. "You guys were always together. I know, you're thinking of Bailey Conners. But she was just a temporary distraction, obviously."

My brain started working on all the input Samantha had just given it, and I quickly steered the conversation away from me and toward her new boyfriend, Brandon. We kept talking about Brandon until I'd finished the page and could tactfully extricate myself.

Most likely to never leave New York? As I walked home, I realized something: I was a little happy that I had been voted for a superlative. But what I was actually happier about, in a weird way, was the fact that I had proven them wrong.

"We have to talk," Callie announced when I got home.

I was surprised at her serious tone. She had treated me with kid gloves since our arrival here, clearly not wanting to upset me or the tenuous truce we had formed. Callie knew I needed her, to finish school, to have a way to live. But I knew she wanted me to stick around for more than just those reasons.

"Okay," I said. "I've got some homework, though. Can we talk later?"

"No. I want to . . . Can we please just talk now?" She began pacing in front of me as I sat on the small love seat that took up a good portion of the living room. I felt my stomach drop a little. I had grown very unfond of news. "I know you aren't going to want to talk to me about this. But I've decided I don't care. I mean, I've decided that no matter the consequences — if you're mad, or even if you decide to leave, that I can't just be quiet anymore."

Whoa. This sounded like a super fun conversation. "What is it?" I asked, not really wanting to hear the answer.

"I can see something here." She continued pacing. "And it's not because I have some special mom powers or some amazing insight into you. I know we're just getting to know each other again." She took a deep breath. "Lexi, I've lived with you for a couple weeks now, I've paid attention. There's something you need to do before you can ever even think of forgiving me, or your father, or even deciding what you're going to do next year."

"What's that?" I asked, afraid suddenly of her insight. I remembered, long ago, not being able to get anything by her.

She took another huge breath, stopping to kneel in front of where I sat. "You need to forgive yourself."

"For what?" I asked, my voice unnaturally loud.

"I think I know, but I'm not sure." She looked at me expectantly.

I sat squirming under her gaze. "I thought I had," I whispered.

"Have you? Then why do you look like you're going to throw up right now?"

"Bad sushi?" I asked, but then gave up the halfhearted

attempt at funny misdirection. "Mom," I started, and barely noted that I'd just used the word for the first time in almost ten years. "I want to. I want to move past it."

"Have you told anybody about it? What you did?"

I shook my head miserably. "It's not even a big deal," I said, feeling pathetic and stupid. "Everyone at school does worse, all the time, before breakfast, even. I'm so pathetic."

"Oh, honey, you're not pathetic!" She leaned forward and put her arms around me. "If you don't want to talk about it, you don't have to. But if you want to tell somebody about it . . . if you want to tell me, I promise I will just listen and then throw it away. Whatever it is, it will pale in comparison to my awfulness. If it makes you feel any better."

I hugged her back. "It might," I admitted and tried to smile.

So I told my mother everything about the night I had betrayed my friend Bailey by fooling around with her boyfriend, betrayed Gavin by not being there on the last night of his life, betrayed myself by doing what I'd done.

She listened and didn't say anything, just made little sounds of comfort or understanding. She interjected nothing at all about Gavin, though she might have wanted to. I thought it would feel awful to look at Callie and know that she knew about the worst thing I'd ever done, but she didn't show any signs of judging me. And I felt lighter, somehow, now that I'd said it all out loud.

As I was heading back to my room, I turned back toward my mom. I was starting to think of her that way again, already. "Mom?"

"What, Lex?"

"You don't have to stay here. It's not that I don't want you to!" I added when I saw her face. "It's just, that's one thing I've learned this year. I think you need to figure out where you belong. Just leave me an address and a phone number — how about that?"

"Deal." Callie smiled, then walked over to me and gave me another hug. "It will all work out," she said in my ear, before releasing me and heading back down the hallway to her room. "Night, Lex," she called over her shoulder. "Love you."

"Love you, too," I called back without thinking.

CHAPTER TWENTY-NINE

SHOULD I STAY OR SHOULD I GO NOW?

"We keep that in mind, that we're older and jaded
We can't shake it"

— THE AMERICAN ANALOG SET, "HARD TO FIND"

Mike's Diner, Bowery—Friday, January 21

"So, the causes leading up to World War I, in order of importance. Go."

"Arrrghh, my brain hurts!" I complained, laying my head dramatically on the table in front of me, narrowly missing the remainder of Eli's eggs.

"You have to pass this, X," he said, using his old nickname for me. Eli's parents had loosened up the house arrest rules a little, and we had been slipping back into a lot of old habits lately, including holding court at our old diner, the one I had been obliged to give up when Bailey found their healthy menu to be lacking.

Eli reached across the table to raise my chin and look directly in my eyes. "You have to study," he told me.

"I know," I said. "I'm going to try to be good. Right after I have some more hot cocoa." I smiled at him.

"Fine," he ground out, grabbing my mug and heading up

to the counter. I was conscious of the fact that I'd just pulled what was essentially a girlfriend move, making him go get my cocoa. Of course, it was a pain to get the waitress's attention when we were in here camping out with books. After half an hour, they basically left us alone, which was great, until we needed something.

I watched Eli at the counter and saw that he hadn't actually had that much trouble getting the attention of the new, young waitress. I felt a little stab of jealousy.

Suddenly I wondered what Nick was doing right now. Probably taking a nap so that he could be handsome and awake for the adoring throng of girls at Revenge later tonight. I tried to quickly change the channel in my brain, looking down at the open textbook before me, but I couldn't quite make my eyes focus on the words. I noticed some egg and coffee stains, though, and wondered if I would have to ask Callie for money to pay for the book at the end of the term.

"Here you go." Eli set my very full mug of cocoa down in front of me.

"Did you forget . . . ?" There were no marshmallows.

Eli grunted. "Who do you think you're dealing with?" he asked, throwing an open bag of mini marshmallows on the table. It was still about half full.

"Wow — marshmallowpalooza. That girl must have really thought you were cute," I observed.

I looked up at him and was surprised to see his cheeks a little pink with embarrassment. "Yeah," was all he said.

"Hmm," I responded. "Well, thanks for that." I broke apart a blob of them — they were kind of melted together — and plopped them in my mug, overflowing the cocoa and adding a new stain to the Causes of World War I chapter.

"You're not really up for studying today, are you?" Eli asked me.

"I thought I was," I told him. "I just feel really distracted."

He nodded. "I know what you mean." He paused. "I got into Columbia."

Why did it feel as though he'd just thrown cold water on my face? "Wow!" I managed. "That's amazing! Go you — but how did you find out this early?"

"Early decision," he told me. "It was my first choice, so I did the binding kind of early decision. So — I'm going. I mean, it's decided."

I closed my breakfast-enhanced history book and reached across the table to take his hands, which were clenched together. "I'm so glad you got in," I told him. "I know that you've always wanted to go there. Of course you'll go there. There's no question. I mean, I was a little worried that Stan was going to send you to community college as punishment, but I guess I should have known that —"

"I want you to go there with me." Eli put his hands around mine and tightened his grip. "I know you applied, and I think you could get in. And I want you to go with me."

I took a deep breath. "I don't know that I will get in," I hedged. I was stalling, and he knew it.

"It doesn't have to be Columbia," he continued in that same patient yet intense voice. "Go to NYU, then. I'd just be uptown. We could meet in the middle. Chelsea, maybe."

I felt his hands, tight around mine. It was hard to breathe.

"What I'm saying is that I want you to stay here, stay with me."

"I . . ." I couldn't speak; there was no air.

I felt him loosen his hold on my hands, but he still held them. Eli started tracing a circle with his thumb, over and over, on the side of my hand. That was making it even harder to think.

"I know you think you were in love with him," he began, not meeting my eyes. "Maybe you really were. And maybe you are still. But he's a good guy, Lexi. He let you go. He knows he's not going in the same direction that you are. But I am. I want to — go where you go."

"But you've already chosen where you're going," I said, my voice very low. His eyes lifted up to meet mine, his mouth opening already in protest or defense. I extricated my hand and raised it palm up. "It's good that you did, it's the right one for you. But, Eli — you're not wanting to walk on *my* path with *me*, you want *me* to go along on *yours*. And I don't know yet — what I want."

"You applied to the University of Miami," he said, and it was kind of an accusation. "I saw the application on your computer."

"I wanted to keep all my options open. I guess I'm waiting for a sign, or inspiration, or . . . something."

"Did you tell *him* you were applying?"

"Yeah. We've just texted a few times."

"What does he say?"

"He said he knows I'll find the right place."

Now that I was back home, it didn't really hurt anymore to think about Nick. It was just kind of nice to know he'd be there if I needed him.

"Well," Eli began, recapturing the hand I'd freed and holding it between both of his. He leaned forward and looked in my eyes. "I wanted you to know that being with me is an option. So consider that while you're deciding, yeah?"

The picture in my head wasn't hard to conjure. Us — Eli and me, meeting up after class, getting coffee, studying, maybe here at this very diner. We could go hear bands on Saturday nights. We could live in a perfect little bubble. Most likely to never leave New York.

I'd only left because I hadn't had a choice. Life had sort of forced me to be brave. Now I was back with a home and a parent, and I had choices again. I didn't have to get on a bus and clean up after an elephant or become a tarot-card reader to survive.

And that's when I realized why I couldn't figure out my future. Even though I'd hated it at the time, I wanted that rush back — I wanted to be scared, I wanted to do something that I never thought I could. But if fate wasn't going to force me into it this time, then it was up to me.

CHAPTER THIRTY

MIDNIGHT CLOWNS

"Well, baby, I'm a put-on-a-show kind of girl"
— BRITNEY SPEARS, "CIRCUS"

Lynchburg, Virginia — Saturday, February 5

Europa looked just the same, even though it was hundreds of miles north of Florida.

Lina and I had both been busy since I'd left, but we'd kept in touch. She'd been updating me on lots of Europa news, but the last time we'd talked she'd hinted about some big news that she wanted to share in person. When she sent me a plane ticket to Virginia, I knew she was serious. Lina picked me up at the airport, we dropped my bag off in my old room in her trailer, and then she pulled me along with her to the ring for her practice.

"You've had quite the effect on my little sister," Lina said, shaking the excess chalk off her hands.

"Where *is* Liska?"

"That's what I was talking about. She quit the act. That's why she's not here. She's staying with a couple of freshmen at the University of Central Florida — like a sleepover orientation or something. She's planning on starting in the fall."

"Seriously? That's great! I mean, it is great, right? But you don't really think it's because of me?" I was trying not to grin too much in case Lina didn't share my glee that Liska was going to go to school.

"Yes, and yes." Lina smiled. "It's totally your fault, but I'm really happy for her. And we'll be cool here once we break in the new girl." Lina cocked her head toward a very young and scared-looking girl wearing a leotard. "Louie found her last week. Name's Katya." Lina dropped her voice to a whisper. "She's completely scared of me. I have no idea why."

Lina shimmied up the rope ladder before I could blink, then hung upside down and grinned at me.

"Yeah, me neither," I said dryly. "So was that the news you wanted to tell me?" I called up to her.

"*Big* news." Upside-down Lina grinned. "You know how Jamie and I have been dating . . ."

I did — Lina'd been updating me about Jamie since Christmas. But I'd predicted the two of them a lot longer ago than that. I hadn't even needed tarot cards.

Lina was sitting right-side up on the swing now. "He asked me to marry him. And I said *yes*!"

"Lina, congratulations! That's amazing." They were so young, but they were also so perfect for each other, I couldn't really be too worried.

"I know, right? Okay, hold on one sec while I show Katya this trick. Katya, watch my arms this time, all right?" Lina swung back and forth a few times, did a double flip in mid-air, then dismounted gracefully off the side of the net. "Did you see what I did there? Now you go." Lina turned to me. "She'll get there. Listen, Lexi, why I really wanted you to come out — I didn't want to ask over the phone. Will you be a bridesmaid?"

"Of course!" I told her, surprised how pleased I felt that she asked. Lina squealed and hugged me.

"When is it? Where is it?"

"May 7! But I haven't really thought about the where part yet. It'll be at home — wherever we are on the show schedule. I'll look it up for you. I'm so glad you're coming!" She hugged me again.

"I wouldn't miss it for anything."

Lina frowned. "There's one other thing I have to tell you. It's about the summer. You remember Nick's mom, right? Madame Tarus?"

I resolved to ignore her mentioning Nick. "She's back with Europa, isn't she?"

"Yes! But Louie will totally hire you for something else. He promised. In fact, you can even be the Go Fish girl if you want!"

"I think that game's a jinx for me," I told her.

"Maybe not. How's Eli, by the way? It's sort of romantic how he came after you and everything. And then you *fainted* . . . just like in a movie."

"Remember when we were never going to bring that up again?"

Lina shook her head and laughed. "Nope. But listen, speaking of your flair for the dramatic, there's one more reason I wanted you to come. There's this thing we're having tonight. We usually have it at the end of the season, but Louie was sick that week, so we moved it to this weekend. It's a circus tradition. Jamie and I have this theory that you'd be pretty good at it."

"What is it?" I asked, suspicious/intrigued.

"You'll see. Listen, I have to work on some more stuff with Katya, but I'll see you at home . . . at my trailer in an hour or so? I'll fill you in then."

I walked through the maze of trailers, and most of the people I passed said hi to me. For once I wasn't in a hurry to get to one of my circus jobs, and I looked around. It was so familiar, even though I'd never been to this town before. I thought about how easy it was for Lina to disregard geography, though the rest of us were its prisoners. She didn't really know — or care — where her wedding would be. She referred to "home," but it wasn't a place she referred to; it was Jamie, and Louie, and her sister, and even her brother, and the rest of the Europa show people. I guessed maybe that was the key — to figure out *who* your home was and find a way to keep them with you.

Jamie was waiting for me on the steps of Lina's trailer.

"Hey, city girl." He smiled. "I hear you're going to do Midnight Clowns."

"And I hear congratulations are in order," I told him, and hugged him. "Wait, I'm going to do *what*?"

"Midnight Clowns. Remember when you promised?"

"I never . . . *ohh* . . ." Lina's evil plan was becoming clear.

Jamie grinned. "Coming back to you now, is it?"

It was.

It was November, and Jamie had tricked me into saying yes to Midnight Clowns — the last night of the season, when the circus gets turned upside down. The crew and backstage people go out into the ring and put on a show, while the performers sit and watch. When Jamie had asked me, I'd protested first that I *had* a show with the Fortune Trailer. He said no way, I was still midway crew, like him.

He'd asked me what I wanted to do, and told me that the whole point of Midnight Clowns is to make fun of the show people. So I'd opened my mouth like an idiot and said I could do some impressions, maybe. All that time I'd spent people-watching during my solo summer in New York had made me kind of observant.

"Impressions of who?" He'd raised an eyebrow.

"Whoever," I'd told him. "How about this one?" I'd stepped a few paces away from him and reached down into an imaginary bucket of chalk. When I straightened my shoulders, I stood far, far straighter than I normally would, as if an invisible iron rod ran through me, and I very precisely coated my hands with the imaginary chalk, sucking in my cheeks a little as if the chalk displeased me.

I stopped when I heard Jamie burst out laughing. "Oh my God — that's the *perfect* Liska. You *have* to do Midnight Clowns. That's hysterical! Can you do more?"

I'd dropped the iron rod, began chewing some imaginary gum, and rolled the sleeves of my T-shirt over my imaginary guns. I leaned against the side of the novelties wagon where we stood, then looked Jamie up and down through hooded eyes. "Hey," was all I said.

I'd watched his eyes grow larger. "You can't do me! I mean, I'm not in the show. You can't make fun of me. But that was pretty good," he added grudgingly.

"You just asked if I could do more." I smiled sweetly. "You didn't specify who."

"Well, figure out who else — who else *from the show* — you wanna do an impersonation of. You should do at least three," he'd explained, and I'd nodded.

"Okay, I'll do it."

"So who are you going to do?" Jamie's question brought me back to the present.

"That was a long time ago — I'm not with the crew anymore!" I protested. "It wouldn't be right!"

"Oh, come on, Lexi. This is a small show. Everyone remembers you. You have to do it. You promised. Besides, it's what Lina and I want for our wedding present." He folded his arms across his chest and smiled smugly. He knew he had me. After all, I was a sucker for a stupid romantic happy ending.

I stood in the center of the ring, my heart beating so loudly, I was kind of afraid I might actually die. I wanted to run out of there and just buy Lina and Jamie a blender or something.

Everyone's eyes were on me, so I did the only thing I could think to do. I closed my eyes, and when I opened them, I was a different person, someone much braver. I sauntered over to the chalk bucket, slathered some on, then very dramatically shook off the extra. It was then that I started to hear the laughing. I kept going, turning to the rope ladder that led up to the trapeze. I began to climb, being sure to add that certain something that Lina always put into her ascent. I knew I couldn't take this impersonation too far — couldn't actually perform on the trapeze, because, suicide. So I stopped climbing and called for Jamie, hearing Lina's voice in my head and matching the pitch and tone.

"Jamie, hey. . . . this rigging feels kinda wrong. Will you fix it?" I batted my eyelashes toward an imaginary Jamie and heard a roar of laughter from the crowd in return.

Jamie actually came forward then, lifted me down. I played along, having to work hard not to laugh myself. Then Jamie grabbed my hand and we bowed quickly together, before he ran off to rejoin Lina. She was sitting there with tears running down her face; she was still laughing. She gave me a huge grin and a thumbs-up sign. It was all the encouragement I needed.

I portrayed Louie next, and he obliged by throwing me his top hat. The crew especially seemed to love that one. I did Faina, the tightrope walker, pretending that the rope was too slack as an excuse for not going up, prancing up to the real Louie with my hands on my hips, complaining and blaming him for the weather and the direction my trailer was facing. "I wanted it north-northwest!" I found Faina in the crowd and was relieved to see she was laughing, too.

I took one more quick bow and ran off to lots of clapping. Nearly everyone I knew came up to congratulate me and tell me how funny I had been.

That was when it hit me. That night I figured out what scared me — made me feel alive. I realized that I wanted to learn how to be an actor, perform like I had that night, only better. Be sort of the opposite of invisible, and hear people clapping for *me*.

And what better place to learn that than New York?

CHAPTER THIRTY-ONE

ALWAYS

"When you gonna realize it was just that the time was wrong, Juliet?"
— DIRE STRAITS, "ROMEO AND JULIET"

202 Delancey Street — Tuesday, March 8

The little yellow room was pitch-black when I walked inside. I thought for one moment, wistfully, of the room I'd left behind just a few blocks away, the one I'd never see again. I hadn't always been happy there, but it had been home. I fumbled for the light switch in the dark; I'd tried first where it had been in the old room.

"Hi," Eli said from the fire escape.

I squeaked in surprise — luckily managing not to scream and bring Callie running. I opened my mouth to say something sarcastic about stalking, but as I watched him stand up and take a step toward me, the words died, and I was just glad to see him.

I closed the small distance between us and put my arms around his chest, under his arms. Eli hesitated for just a fraction of a second, then his arms closed around me, too, and he squeezed tight. I heard him say my name, almost a whisper.

Somehow, my confession to Callie had changed the way this felt, being in Eli's arms. It didn't feel wrong or bad anymore. In fact, it felt pretty much perfect.

"Happy to see me?" he asked in my ear.

"Always." I smiled against his chest. "Well, maybe not *historically* always, but . . . I think maybe from now on . . . always."

Eli pulled back just enough to look down at my face. "Do you mean that? Because it's always for me, too. Has been for a long time."

"I mean it," I told him. And it was true.

I still loved Nick — some part of me always would. But now I felt free to love Eli again, too. I'd forgiven myself for what I'd done. And now that I knew — really knew — what it felt like to love two people, I could forgive Eli for last year, too.

Eli pulled me with him to the window seat, pulling me down into his lap. "I missed you," he said simply, and I knew what he meant. Even though we'd been with each other the last few months, it hadn't been like it was, hadn't been like this.

"I missed you, too."

"So, about next year . . ." Eli started.

"Not sure yet," I told him. "There's sort of an idea I had, that I've been working on . . ."

"In New York?"

"Hey! Slow down — I'm not telling you yet. But either way, it doesn't have to mean the end of you and me. You know that, right? Wherever we go for college, we'll still have each other."

"I guess so," Eli grumbled. "I'd just like to have you in New York." He kind of growled that last part in my ear, and I couldn't help myself — I giggled.

"Well, we'll just have to wait and see what happens. For tonight, you gotta go. Stan will murder you if you're out all night, and then we really won't be in the same place."

"You mean you wouldn't pull a Juliet to stay with me for all eternity?"

I got up and pulled him to his feet, shoving him toward the fire escape. "Would you want me to?" I asked him.

"No." Eli put his arms on my shoulders. "I really just want you to be happy, Lexi. I mean, I want you with me. But I want you to be happy more."

I leaned forward and kissed him. It was a soft, quick kiss, the first one since *that* night. Eli looked surprised, but he smiled.

"Thank you, by the way," I told him.

"For what?"

"For coming to find me at Europa. I know I wasn't happy to see you at the time. But I was still glad you came for me."

"I'll always come for you," Eli said, sounding serious again. "So just remember that — if you decide to go away. That I'll always come for you." With that he was out the window and down the stairs. Gone, but only for the night.

EPILOGUE

"I need to break out and make a new name
Let's open our eyes to the brand-new day"
— RYAN STAR, "BRAND NEW DAY"

The Corner of Broadway and Waverly—Tuesday, September 6

"Well, this is it," I said, clutching my class schedule in one hand and Eli's hand in the other.

"Do you have everything?" he asked me for about the fifth time.

"I think so. I mean, I think I'm ready."

"I think you are, too." Eli smiled and squeezed my hand. "So I'll be uptown if you need me. And after classes today we'll —"

"Meet in the middle . . . I know." I smiled. The middle, for now, was a hole-in-the-wall diner in Chelsea that kind of reminded us both of Mike's. Eli had ended up with a pretty great scholarship for Columbia, so Stan had agreed to foot the bill for a dorm room.

I was going to be living in a dorm, too. I'd gotten the one letter of acceptance that I really wanted, to the Tisch Institute

of Performing Arts. Even applying to Tisch had been scary —
I couldn't just fill out the paperwork and send it in. I'd
actually had to audition. I'd used a scene from *The Tempest*,
which I'd read so many times during the downtime at
Europa. And then I'd sweated it out all spring until I finally
got the news: I was accepted.

Callie was surprised, and I think kind of impressed. She
hadn't known I had it in me. Neither had I.

I'd had to work on her for months to get her to feel okay
about leaving, but finally she understood that I was trying to
keep her in my life, but I was doing it by setting her free. She
hated being stuck in one place, and I knew it. And there was
no reason for her to hang around the city while I got sucked
into life and school. Callie was headed to San Francisco, and
we made a deal to meet back up for Christmas, and to spend
the next summer together.

Eli kissed me and said good-bye, and I started walking
toward the doors of the main building on 721 Broadway.

As I was opening the door, I felt my phone buzz in my
pocket. I took it out and read the message from Nick.

BREAK A LEG AT TISCH, CIRCUS GIRL :)

I smiled and I texted back that I planned to.

It was almost ten hours later when I let myself into my new
dorm room. I had won a lottery for a single room somehow — which was pretty lucky, since Eli had two roommates
at Columbia this semester.

Today had been a blur of embarrassing theater exercises,

being thrown into scenes that were tragic, funny, and everything in between, with people I'd just met. We'd all gone out to lunch together, laughing like war buddies already, everyone getting nicknames. Mine was DJ, since I'd known the title and artist of every song that had played at the diner during lunch. I didn't tell anyone why that name was sort of ironic, yet cool — that my dad had been an actual DJ. It was still too soon, but I knew it wouldn't be forever. I felt accepted there already.

And then it was time to meet Eli in the middle.

I pushed open the door to our in-between place, and he was already waiting for me. He stood up at the booth he'd been saving and gave me this huge smile. I hugged him hard when I got to the table.

"Did it go okay?" I heard the concern in his voice.

I leaned back to look up at him. "It went awesome. How about you?"

He smiled. "Awesome. So, what are you having?"

I sat down beside him in the booth. I hadn't traveled that far — not yet. You could measure how far I was from my old life in blocks. But the path to get here had led all the way to Florida and back. And it had taken a lot to make it to Eli's side of the booth, sitting close by him — together.

"So how do you think the waffles are here?" I asked him.

ACKNOWLEDGMENTS

I am so grateful to my fantastic editor, Aimee Friedman: Without you, none of this would have been possible. Thank you so much for your guidance, your great ideas, and most of all for believing in me and in this story.

Mom and Dad, thank you for instilling a love of reading in me early on, starting with that big bucket of Golden Books. And to my talented brother, Jim: Thank you for designing such a great website for me. I love you guys.

Thank you to Nikki Morrell, for reading this story many (many) times, in every incarnation, and for generally being my best friend.

My chicas — Nik, Carolla, and Beth — thanks and love for always being there to laugh with me.

Thank you to Angela Im and Arlene Robillard: I haven't met you yet, but I will be forever grateful for your help in getting my book its ticket to NYC.

My professors at Tiffin, Vince and Lee: Thanks for reading this book early on and giving great advice (like *add more circus*!).

My students — past, present, and future — for inspiring me, helping me speak teen, and being excited about this project. A special shout-out has to go to Gaby C, and she knows why.

Finally, a huge thank-you to everyone at Scholastic who read this story, believed in me, and helped make this idea a reality.